Terror at FORBIDDEN FALLS

Lee Roddy

PUBLISHING
Colorado Springs, Colorado

Terror at
FORBIDDEN FALLS

TERROR AT FORBIDDEN FALLS

Copyright 1993 by Lee Roddy

Library of Congress Cataloging-in-Publication Data

Roddy, Lee, 1921—
    Terror at Forbidden Falls / Lee Roddy.

        p.   cm. — (A Ladd Family adventure)
        Summary: A dangerous adventure begins for the Ladds when mammoth waves hit Oahu
and they rescue a father and daughter in very strange circumstances.
        ISBN 1-56179-137-7

        [1. Mystery and detective stories.   2. Hawaii—Fiction   3. Christian life—Fiction]
I. Title.   II. Series: Roddy, Lee, 1921—   Ladd Family adventure.
PZ7.R6Tc   1993
[Fic]—dc20   93-3379
                                                                                      CIP
                                                                                      AC

Published by Focus on the Family Publishing, Colorado Springs, CO 80995.
Distributed by Word Books, Waco, Texas.

Scripture quotations are taken from the Holy Bible, New International Version copyright
1973, 1978, International Bible Society.

The author is represented by the literary agency of Alive Communications, P.O. Box 49068,
Colorado Springs, Colorado 80949

Editor: Ron Klug
Cover Illustration: Ernest Norcia
Printed in the United States of America
، 94 95 96 97 98 99/ 10 9 8 7 6 5 4 3 2

For Lois Spelmann,
whose friendship has always been there
for my family and me,
and in loving memory of
Dr. Lyle Spelmann

CONTENTS

Chapter One

THE MONSTER WAVE

In all his 12 years of life, Josh Ladd had never seen such a stormy night. He glanced anxiously at his father, who gripped the steering wheel and strained to see through the windshield. The wiper blades beat uselessly against the sheets of semitropical downpour.

To the right, and less than a hundred yards away that Tuesday night, the Pacific Ocean was visible only as a vast, black mass with flickers of whitecaps. The streetlights swayed in the violent winds. Inland, to the left, Josh could make out the faint glow of lights in houses that had been hastily abandoned. It wasn't cold, although it was the week between Christmas and New Year's.

Trying to swallow a lump of fear in his throat, Josh asked softly, "We going to make it, Dad?"

John Ladd didn't reply but grimly steered the old, white station wagon along Highway 83 on Oahu's* North Shore. Josh turned to see how his best friend was doing in the back seat.

"Look!" Tank Catlett exclaimed, pointing through the windshield.

1

Josh whirled around, his blue eyes probing the night. A flash of sheet lightning lit up the sky, giving a brief glimpse of the road curving slightly seaward. A small cliff momentarily broke the storm's fury so that the headlights shone directly onto the Pacific.

The high beams revealed a normal swell of about two feet that continued to rise. It rapidly became a monstrous wave that rose to six feet, then 12 and was still rising as it rushed shoreward.

Josh cried, "Dad, what's that? A tidal wave?"

"No!" Mr. Ladd jammed his foot down hard, making the vehicle accelerate rapidly as the road straightened out again. "I think it's another of those giant waves that made the authorities order this area evacuated."

"Will it cross the road?"

"Yes! Hang on! I'm going to try to beat it to the safety of that little hill up ahead!"

Josh pivoted to look back as another flash of lightning momentarily turned the night into day. The monster wave was now higher than a house and still rising, towering higher and higher, rushing across the small, sandy beach toward the paved road.

"Faster, Mr. Ladd, faster!" Tank yelled.

"I've got my foot to the floorboard!"

Josh glanced fearfully toward the sea as lightning flashed again. He realized they were passing the giant wave. It was now taller than a two-story building, surging toward the speeding station wagon.

"It's gaining on us!" Josh shouted, watching in horrified fascination. The red glow of the twin taillights reflected off the wave. "It's going to. . . "

Josh's words were snapped off when the wave slammed into the big vehicle. Instantly, it was lifted like a child's toy in a bathtub. Josh instinctively sucked in his breath, but it was knocked out of him as the station wagon slid sideways off the pavement into an embankment.

The headlights shot skyward, vainly probing through the downpour. Then the station wagon bounced crazily, tilted sharply over on its left side, and stopped. Only Josh's seat belt kept him from crashing into his father.

Slowly, the vehicle rocked back upright, making the headlights dance up and down against the rain. In their beams, Josh glimpsed the horrifying sight of the surging seawater rushing past the car and up the hill to where the black pavement blended with the night.

There the foaming water slowed, stopped, then drained rapidly back. The headlights reappeared as the retreating water surged past the windshield and the vehicle's top. The motor died, but the headlights stayed on. Josh's eyes followed the receding water by the taillights until it left the road and the beach reappeared.

"Whew!" Josh breathed, "That was close!"

"You're telling me!" Tank muttered weakly.

"Thank God," Mr. Ladd whispered as the car settled onto all four wheels. He added, "You boys all right?"

"I . . . I think so," Josh replied.

"Same here," Tank answered, "except I've been scared out of a year's growth."

Mr. Ladd instructed, "Unbuckle your seat belts while I get my door open. Hurry before another wave hits!"

Josh needed no urging. He unsnapped his belt and slid toward his father. In the reflected glow of the dashboard lights, Josh saw the door open. His father's hand closed on his left wrist and pulled him forward and out of the station wagon.

Josh's bare feet sank into a muddy ditch by the roadside. The downpour instantly drenched the boy's cutoff blue jeans and green tee shirt. His wavy dark hair flattened across his blue eyes.

Mr. Ladd helped Tank get the back door open and assisted the boy to the ground. "Come on!" Mr. Ladd cried above the drumming sound of the rain on the station wagon's roof. "Let's get to high ground!"

He sloshed out of the muddy ditch and onto the glistening-wet pavement. Josh and Tank splashed after him, running up the center of the road where it rose in the headlights.

They reached the crest of the hill before Mr. Ladd stopped and looked back. "I think we're safe now, boys."

Panting from his brief, hard run, Josh looked back at a strange sight. The station wagon's lights were still on. So were the streetlights. Electricity inside empty homes showed that power was still on there, too.

Josh's dad said, "I think the rain's slowing up."

Josh nodded, catching his breath and letting his gaze

sweep the scene below. It was quiet because everyone had been evacuated when Hawaii authorities had spread the warning about expected mammoth waves on the North Shore.

Mr. Ladd said, "They were calling this the storm of the century, although the last one was in 1969. There wasn't supposed to be another one for about the next hundred years."

Josh, feeling considerable relief, commented, "There's a house over there on the side of the hill. Everybody's been evacuated, but maybe we can get in and use their phone. . . . " He broke off his sentence when he heard a loud cracking noise of splintering wood.

The front of the house suddenly dipped and started to slide downhill with a sound of breaking glass and the groan of wood being ripped apart.

Like many Hawaiian homes, it had been built off the ground with wooden lattice work around the bottom. Josh guessed the monster wave had slipped under it, loosening the foundation. The house moved only a foot or so downhill before the water retreated to the sea. The house, free of its foundation, teetered precariously.

"Look!" Josh exclaimed, pointing to the near window. "There are people in there!"

"I see them!" Tank cried. "Two men! They're running toward the back door."

Seconds later, the door opened and the men dashed out into the night. One was of medium build and ran faster than the other, who was heavyset, with a potbelly that protruded over his belt. They sprinted to a dark sedan parked in the rutted dirt driveway. Car doors slammed, and the headlights came on.

As the motor sprang to life, Mr. Ladd said hopefully, "Maybe they'll give us a ride into Honolulu."* He started to step into the roadway.

But the car shot out of the driveway at an unsafe speed, fishtailed as it swung onto the wet pavement, and accelerated uphill toward the soaking wet man and boys.

Mr. Ladd waved his arms and moved forward so he'd be clearly seen in the oncoming headlights, but the car didn't slow.

"Dad, look out!" Josh shouted, jumping back and almost tripping over Tank. "They're not going to stop!"

The sedan swerved around the trio with an angry blast of the horn, then raced away into the night.

"Not very friendly," Tank observed in his slow, easy way. "Where's their aloha spirit?"*

"I never would have expected anybody to leave us out here like this," Josh admitted.

His father commented, "There's something strange about their behavior, all right." He turned back toward the house.

Josh did the same, then stopped and grabbed his father's arm in sudden excitement. "Dad, somebody else is in there! I just saw them pass the window!"

He broke off as another monster wave thundered across the road below them, smashed into the house, and started dragging it seaward. The electric lines to the home snapped with a shower of sparks, plunging the home into total darkness.

The house gained momentum as it slid off the hill and scooted across the roadway on the crest of the retreating wave. The front end of the dwelling smashed into a telephone pole, causing an electrical display and another shower of sparks. Then the streetlights blinked out along with all those in the neighboring houses. Except for the station wagon's lights, there was sudden, total darkness everywhere else.

Then a scream came through the blackness.

Josh's father cried, "That sounded like a woman!" He started running down the slanting pavement. "I'm going to help her before the whole house goes into the ocean!"

"I'm coming with you, Dad!" Josh shouted, starting to run after his father. "Come on, Tank!"

Behind him, Tank groaned in dismay as Mr. Ladd called over his shoulder. "No! You boys stay here! Another wave might sweep you away!"

Josh slowed to obey, then started running again as someone shouted from inside the house.

"Dad!" Josh cried. "That's a man's voice! There's somebody else in the house besides the woman we heard. You'll need help getting them both out."

Mr. Ladd didn't answer, so Josh sprinted after him, anxiously glancing seaward, fearful of seeing another monster wave rushing shoreward.

As Josh and Tank raced past the station wagon and out of its light, they stopped in bewilderment when the sudden contrast with the night blinded them. Then, as quickly as they could, they stumbled on to where the bulk of the wrecked house showed faintly against the horizon.

Josh suddenly remembered that live wires might have been knocked into the puddles, threatening them with instant electrocution. But before he could shout a warning, Josh heard a faint cry from the house.

"Help!" It was the feminine voice. "Somebody help!"

Josh forgot about the possibility of being electrocuted. He followed his father toward the sound.

By the time they reached the back part of the house, which extended over the center dividing line in the roadway, the rain had slackened considerably. Josh's eyes had adjusted to the darkness. Another flash of lightning showed movement ahead.

"There, Dad!" Josh pointed. "At the back door!"

"I see them! You boys help the woman! I'll get the man!"

The victims had staggered into the roadway when Josh, his father, and Tank rushed upon the scene. Josh reached out and grabbed for the woman's bare arm. "Here! I've got you! Tank, take her other arm and let's get out of here!"

"No! I'm okay! Let go!" the feminine voice replied sharply. She struggled to free her arms. "Help my father! He's hurt!"

"My dad will take care of him," Josh assured her, tightening his grip on her slippery wet forearm.

The lightning flashed again, giving Josh a glimpse of chestnut hair flattened by rain over the woman's face, completely covering it. Josh also saw his father pulling the man's left arm over Mr. Ladd's right shoulder. The man sagged weakly, his head forward.

"You boys take her and get up to the crest of that hill!" Mr. Ladd commanded. "I can manage this one."

Nodding in the darkness, Josh and Tank led the struggling, protesting victim away and up the hill.

Silently, Josh prayed, *O Lord, don't let another wave come in before we get to safety!*

As Josh stumbled past the station wagon, the headlights gave him his first glimpse of the person he was half-dragging, half-leading toward safety.

"A girl!" he exclaimed in surprise

"Of course I'm a girl!" she replied sharply.

"I thought I heard a woman's voice . . ."

"There's only Dad and me! Now, let go of me! I can take care of myself!" She again tried to squirm free of the boys' grip. "I've got to help my father!"

"No, Melanie!" the injured man spoke for the first time. His voice was weak. "Stay there!"

The name of Melanie struck a raw nerve in Josh's memory, but he shook off the thought and finished leading the now compliant girl up the crest of the hill, where the headlights blended with the night.

For the first time, he got a quick look at the girl. She was slender, wearing white shorts and a blue halter top. Her face was still hidden under the water-matted hair.

Josh stopped, puffing from exertion, and released her. She swung around, twisted free from Tank's grip, and started running back down the hill.

"Dumb girl!" Tank grumbled.

Josh was inclined to think she was stubborn, but he defended her. "She's just concerned about her father. I'll go get her."

As he started running, with Tank following, Josh saw that his dad was supporting the girl's father.

The man called, "Stay there, Melanie! I'm all right!"

She obeyed, but when the two men were within a few feet, she hurried forward. The headlights cast her shadow over Josh. "Oh, Daddy!" she cried, as Mr. Ladd released the man's right arm. He stood a little unsteadily in the roadway as his daughter threw her arms around his neck. "I was so scared!"

"We all were," he assured her, stroking her wet hair. He looked at Josh, Mr. Ladd, and Tank. "You risked your lives for strangers. Not many would do that."

Mr. Ladd said with forced lightness, "Well, everyone else is evacuated. I'm just glad the boys and I were here to help. You badly hurt, sir?"

"I'll be all right, thanks." Still holding the girl with his left arm, he reached out with his right. "I'm Brad Redcliff," he said, shaking hands with Mr. Ladd. "This is my daughter, Melanie."

Josh jerked as though he'd been shocked.

The girl also reacted, suddenly reaching up to brush the hair out of her eyes. Her brown eyes darted from one to the other, then she stared straight at Josh.

Tank whispered, "Oh, no! It can't be!"

None of the others seemed to notice as Josh's father said, "I'm John Ladd. This is my son Josh and his friend Tank Catlett."

Melanie's father, obviously concerned about the danger, did not acknowledge the introduction. Instead, he said, "We'd better get out of here. Those two men will be back."

He paused, then added somberly, "I'm sorry, but the fact that you three showed up here probably means that you're now in danger too."

Chapter Two

MYSTERY OF THE PONO PAHA

Josh swallowed hard as a bitter taste seeped into his mouth. Melanie Redcliff had entered his life again. As before, she was making his life miserable.

"Why are *we* in danger?" Josh's dad asked Melanie's father.

He said, "I'll tell you on the way out of here. Is that your station wagon down there, Mr. Ladd?"

"Yes," Josh's father replied just as the lights dimmed and went out. "But the motor died when a giant wave caught us from behind. There go my lights. They must have shorted out, so the battery and wiring are surely too wet for me to get it started again."

"Then we'll have to walk," Brad Redcliff announced firmly in the darkness. "Give me your hand, Melanie."

"But you're hurt, Dad!" she protested.

"We don't have a choice, Honey," he said somberly. "Those two men ran when the wave hit the house, but I'm sure they'll be back."

13

"Why are they after you?" Mr. Ladd asked, leading the way down the road toward Honolulu. "And how did we get involved in this?"

Redcliff didn't answer directly, but asked, "Did those men see you three as they drove away?" When Josh's father nodded, Redcliff continued, "Then they'll figure you're all witnesses to what happened to Melanie and me, and they can't afford to leave any witnesses. We have to get off this highway before they come back. Is there a side road around here?"

"I don't know," Mr. Ladd answered. "We don't drive this way very often. I own a tourist publication in Waikiki,* so we'd driven around to Kahuku Point* to interview a man for my publication. It's much shorter driving back by way of Sunset Beach than it is to take Highway 83 down to Kaneohe* and across the Koolau Range,* so we came this way along the North Shore."

"Yeah!" Tank said in the darkness. "But we didn't expect to see any waves crossing the highway."

"It's a good thing you did come this way," Redcliff replied. He waited while the sound of another mammoth wave smashed ashore and lightning flashed.

Josh heard Melanie gasp as the wave crushed the wooden house and swept it into the ocean along with palm fronds, picnic benches, and other debris.

"Otherwise," Redcliff continued, "Melanie and I might now be out there in the Pacific with what's left of that house."

He paused, then added, "I'm afraid that if those men return, they'll treat you and the boys the same way they treated me. Fortunately, they didn't touch Melanie, although they threatened her."

When the sky lit up again, instead of looking for another road, Josh looked straight at the girl, remembering what she had done last year in California.

She met his gaze firmly and smiled, but it wasn't a friendly smile. There was something cold and hard about it that Josh had seen before. The last time was on the Mainland when she had triumphantly accepted a scholarship pin that he was sure he really should have received.

She cheated! he told himself as darkness again settled over the group. *Just as she did the first time! Now our lives are in danger because we tried to help her!*

Melanie's father spoke again, breaking into Josh's thoughts. "We have to get off this road, yet we don't dare go toward the beach because of those terrible waves. I know there's a side road somewhere near here, along with some other houses on the left. But I'm disoriented, so everybody be ready when the lightning flashes again. Try to find a way off this highway."

Mr. Ladd said, "There hasn't been another car pass here, so the police must have blocked the highway."

"That's likely," Redcliff agreed. "But if those men get over their fright before they reach the roadblock, they'll turn back to search for us. They're trying to stop me from writing a story I'm working on. You see, we received a call at our Honolulu hotel, that a man would be at this house to give me the information I wanted. I let Melanie ride along.

"But when we arrived here, the house was empty. Then those two men arrived, tied us up, and threatened us. That big wave scared them off. But if they come back . . ."

Redcliff left the sentence unfinished as lightning flashed again. Josh saw that the man limped slightly.

Melanie added, "We had just freed ourselves when the house started sliding toward the ocean."

"What story were you working on?" Mr. Ladd asked.

"It's about . . ."

"Car coming!" Tank interrupted.

"It's them!" Melanie whispered in a frightened voice. "Oh, Dad! If they catch us again . . ."

She let her thought trail off as lighting flashed in the distance. Josh looked quickly to his left. "There! I saw a house with a driveway. I'll lead the way."

Guided by the memory of the momentary glimpse he'd had of a darkened home, Josh moved forward. He and Tank were barefooted even though it was winter in Hawaii. Their feet were noiseless on the wet pavement in sharp contrast to the sound of leather shoes worn by the two men and the girl.

Josh found a narrow gravel driveway that hurt his feet, but that was the least of his concerns. He picked his way past rustling banana leaves and the fragrance of plumeria,* which blooms year-round in Hawaii. The house was in total darkness, but everyone followed the walls around to the back lanai.*

"We'll be able to see those men if they drive up here," Redcliff explained. "In the meantime, we can watch them without being seen."

"If they turn into this driveway," Josh's father added, "let's head straight out back. By the lightning, I saw that there's a little valley planted in sugarcane. We'll be able to hide there."

Tank leaned close to Josh and whispered, "Are you thinking what I'm thinking?"

Josh whispered back, "You mean that we're in all this trouble because of her?"

"Yeah! We know she cheated you out of that scholarship pin. But we helped save her life, and look at the mess we're in!"

"Shh!" Josh hissed as a car's headlights, moving slowly, drew even with the watchers.

There was a tense silence when nobody spoke. In the distance, Josh heard the explosive crash of giant waves as they repeatedly assaulted the shore. Hawaii's temperate climate, even in winter, was so mild that the survivors were not cold, but only uncomfortable, from their wet clothes.

"They're passing!" Josh said with a sigh of relief. He watched as the headlights topped the hill, where the station wagon rested out of sight.

Seconds later Josh's father said softly, "Their lights stopped moving. Since your house has been washed out to sea, those men are probably inspecting our vehicle. They'll find the registration and learn my name and address. They'll know where to find us."

"I'm really sorry," Redcliff said softly.

Mr. Ladd said crisply, "Mr. Redcliff, we've waited long enough to find out who those men are and why they're after you."

"And us," Tank added in a hoarse whisper.

"Well, I'm a magazine feature writer. My publication sent me to Hawaii to do a piece on the mysterious disappearance of certain ancient artifacts from the museum in Honolulu."

"I thought your name sounded familiar," Mr. Ladd exclaimed. "I've seen your byline. You're a good writer."

"Thanks. I was following up on those disappearances when I stumbled upon a bigger story."

"I'll say!" Melanie added. "Dad tried to get an interview with Mano* of the Pono Paha."* She paused, then asked, "You've heard of him?"

"Who hasn't?" Tank asked in his slow, easy way, but there was an edge to his words. "Mano means shark in Hawaiian."

Melanie ignored Tank. "Dad's investigation found a connection between the museum thefts and the Pono Paha. Do you boys know what that means?"

Josh sensed a tinge of haughtiness in her question. He stopped staring at the distant glow of stopped headlights to turn toward Melanie in the darkness. "Yes, we do. Pono Paha is Hawaiian for 'is that right?' The man called Mano is the leader of that radical group."

"Josh is right," his father added. "These islands are involved in the emotionally charged kanaka maoli* movement. These 'true Hawaiian's,' like the Indians on the Mainland, want a more equitable distribution of the land than they now have.

"As you know, in January of 1893, U.S. Marines dethroned the last native queen, Liliuokalani,* and overthrew the Hawaiian monarchy. Without sovereignty,* the kanaka maoli have no right to sue in either state or federal courts for lands they believe were stolen from them. Most native Hawaiians are reasonable and willing to work things out, but Pono Paha leads a radical element that demands absolute sovereignty be restored. Mano and his followers also want all foreigners expelled from Hawaii, and not just us haoles.* Mano advocates civil disobedience and even violence to achieve their goals."

Tank added, "And we know a kid at school who wishes he was old enough to join them—Kamuela* Kong. Only we call him King Kong after the gorilla movie monster."

Josh squirmed uncomfortably, recalling the many unpleasant encounters he'd had with the school bully. "Kong hates all us haoles," Josh observed. "He'd like to kick us all out . . ." He broke off suddenly to exclaim, "That car's turning around!"

Mr. Redcliff said grimly, "Since they didn't find us along the highway, they'll probably start searching the houses."

"And this is the first one," Tank muttered. "Come on, Josh. Let's head for the cane field."

"Wait!" Josh exclaimed. "Another car's coming!"

He joined the others in watching the second vehicle. It was headed north at a moderate speed.

"Who could that be?" Melanie asked quietly.

"I've no idea," her father replied. "I just hope it isn't another carload of thugs joining the first two in searching for us."

"Hey!" Josh exclaimed. "The first car turned off its lights."

"That probably means they saw the oncoming headlights, but didn't want to be seen," Redcliff said. He added, "It could be a police car. Who else would be out here except them?"

"Makes sense," Mr. Ladd said. "I hope you're right."

Everyone fell silent as the second car came closer. Josh held his breath, silently praying, *Lord, let it be the police!*

Tank squirmed up close to whisper in Josh's ear. "After what Melanie's done to you, I sort of wish they'd catch her but leave us alone."

"You don't mean that," Josh whispered back. "Those men play rough, judging by what little I could see of her father's face."

"Well, she's a perfect example of why some of the natives want to kick . . . Hey! That *is* a police car!"

Josh nodded. A jagged streak of lightning in the distance had given him enough light that Josh clearly saw it reflected in the distinctive blue lights used on Hawaiian police vehicles.

"It *is!*" Josh cried. "It's the police! Dad, should I run down to the road and flag them down?"

"Sounds like a good idea to me. Mr. Redcliff, do you agree?"

"Certainly! Then we can tell the officers about those thugs, so they can be taken into custody."

"Go on, son!" Mr. Ladd instructed, "but don't fall in the darkness."

Guided by a distant flash of lightning, Josh dashed into the oncoming car's headlights. He frantically waved both arms over his head.

As the police car stopped, the balding haole driver rolled

down his window. His partner was a local* of Japanese-American heritage. Josh blurted out his story.

When Josh had finished, the driver nodded. "We'll check it out."

"Thanks!" Josh exclaimed with great relief. "Thanks a lot! I'll run back to tell my dad and the others."

"No," the haole replied firmly. "You'd better come with us. We don't want to have to start looking for you if this doesn't check out. It won't hurt your father and the others to wait a few minutes. So get in the back seat."

Josh reluctantly slid into the patrol unit, feeling uncomfortable with the strong wire mesh that separated him from the officers. The driver put the car into gear.

I sure hope they catch those guys! Josh thought, turning to look back toward the darkened house where his father and the others waited. Then Josh faced forward again as the police car topped the hill. The headlights showed both the white station wagon and a black sedan.

The local officer activated a powerful spotlight, playing it across the two other vehicles and the area around them. "No sign of anyone," he commented.

"They must have heard you coming and hid someplace," Josh said.

"Maybe," the driver replied. "You sit tight. We'll take a look around."

Josh's anxiety increased as the two officers took their long flashlights and searched both the dark sedan and the white station wagon. They spread out, widening their search while Josh heard the thunderous crashing of the high surf that surged across the narrow beach.

Both policemen walked back to their car and shined their lights into the back seat, making Josh squint.

The driver said bluntly, "Kid, we don't know what to make of your story. We can see where a house washed out to sea, and the two vehicles, but no sign of anyone."

"They have to be close by!" Josh protested, feeling the officers were suspicious of him.

"Maybe," the driver said without conviction, "and maybe not. But they'd be fools to stay where another big wave could catch them. And since we're not fools, we're going to get out of here, fast."

"Don't you believe me?" Josh cried in anguish.

The balding man slid under the steering wheel before answering. "Your story is just weird enough to investigate further. So we'll go pick up your father and the others. Maybe we can get to the bottom of this on the way back to the police station."

"Police station?" Josh asked in a croak. "Am I being arrested?"

"Relax!" The driver's voice was firm as he started turning the vehicle around.

Josh sagged weakly in the back seat, suddenly realizing that he didn't know for sure that anything Mr. Redcliff or his daughter had said was true.

What kind of a mess have I gotten into? Josh asked himself. *What's going to happen now?*

Chapter Three

ECHOES FROM THE PAST

The two officers pulled into the driveway where Josh's father and the others waited, soaking wet from the warm storm. Everyone excitedly asked questions of Josh and the policemen as they exited the car.

The balding driver raised his voice and took charge. "We'll ask the questions," he said, flipping his flashlight to each of the five persons. "We'll fill out a field interrogation report, so everyone settle down and we'll get through this as quickly as possible."

Josh found himself trembling with excitement when the questions were completed. "Now do you believe me?" he asked the balding officer.

The policeman turned off his flashlight. "This whole issue of sovereignty has aroused both the kanaka maoli who are reasonable, along with some radicals who aren't," the haole officer answered. "The two men who assaulted Mr. Redcliff and his daughter sound like two muscle men known to our department from the Pono Paha splinter faction."

"Oh?" Redcliff asked. "What're their names?"

"We don't have rap sheets on them, but the driver who ran to the car so fast sounds like a man known on the streets only as Holo.* The other attacker with the potbelly sounds like one locally called Opu Nui."*

"That means Big Belly," Josh said, "if I remember my Hawaiian words correctly."

"Close enough," the officer said with a smile. "But if these *are* the two men who attacked Mr. Redcliff and his daughter, they're dangerous."

Melanie exclaimed in a frightened whisper, "You're not going to leave us out here, are you? Those men could be hiding someplace, waiting for you two to leave us."

"All seven of us can't ride in this patrol unit," he replied. "So let's see if we can get your station wagon started."

He invited Josh, Tank, and Melanie to ride in the back seat with him. The other officer took his flashlight and walked with the two fathers.

Josh felt very uncomfortable with Melanie sitting between him and Tank. But Tank asked her, "You still have that scholarship pin from last year at school?"

"Yes," she answered sharply, "but I won it!"

Tank snorted, "You didn't win it! Josh did! You know that, so why don't you give it back?"

"Are you saying I cheated?" Melanie demanded hotly, whirling to face Tank.

Before he could answer, Josh said, "Forget it."

The girl turned toward him. "I can't forget it when you

two obviously haven't."

Josh didn't answer, but Melanie was right. He held a strong resentment toward her, not just because she had received a pin he honestly believed he had won, but because he was sure she had cheated in winning. He didn't like cheats. He didn't like the danger to which he, his father, and Tank had been exposed by trying to help Melanie and her father. Yet Josh realized that if anything happened to Melanie, he would be very sorry.

The officers were unable to get Mr. Ladd's station wagon started, so they radioed for a tow truck. However, since there wouldn't be room in the truck's cab for all five of them, a taxi was also called. The policemen stayed until the two vehicles arrived.

As the policemen started to drive away, Josh and the others crowded around to thank them. Mr. Ladd said, "I found my vehicle registration on the ground, so those men obviously know my address. Do you think I should send my family someplace else for awhile?"

"We can't advise you on that, sir," the driver replied, starting the patrol car's motor. "Detectives will contact you and follow up our report."

Josh and Tank, still wet from the rain, slid into the taxi's front seat with the driver. Melanie and the two fathers sat in back. The taxi followed the officers' taillights along Highway 83 toward Haleiwa.*

As they rolled past pineapple fields and sugar cane plantations, Redcliff said, "Melanie, I'm going to send you back to the Mainland as soon as I can book a flight. I'll stay here and follow up on this story."

Melanie protested. "I want to stay here with you."

"Sorry, sweetheart, but it's not safe."

Tank muttered so softly only Josh could hear, "The sooner she's gone, the better."

Josh felt himself wanting to intervene on Melanie's behalf, and that surprised him. But he managed to keep his thoughts to himself.

He leaned toward Tank and whispered, "I'm more concerned about those two men the police called Holo and Opu Nui. Are you?"

"Yeah."

Josh glanced back to see if anyone seemed to be following them. Satisfied, he tried to sound confident. "I think things will be okay."

"Well, I'm not," Tank answered glumly.

Josh smiled at his friend. "Why must you always look at the dark side of things?" he teased.

"I'm just being practical," Tank insisted.

Josh didn't answer, but turned to listen to the conversation from the back seat. His eyes caught Melanie's, and he stirred uneasily and looked away.

The conflict within him made him squirm. *What's the matter with me?* he scolded himself and forced his attention to his father's words.

Mr. Ladd had been a high-school history teacher on the Mainland. This, combined with his present position as publisher of an Hawaiian tourist publication, made him knowledgeable about the state's current unrest.

"I'm sure, Mr. Redcliff, that . . ."

"Call me Brad."

"Brad, I'm John. Anyway, I'm sure that in researching the story for your magazine, you've learned quite a bit about the current unrest in this state."

"Oh, yes, but I'm always eager to learn more."

"Well, it's my understanding that only a few of the native Hawaiian people are demanding independence or restoration of the monarchy that U.S. Marines overthrew on January 17, 1893.

"However, strong and widespread support exists for some redress of grievances. The Pono Paha is probably the most radical of those groups who want to go back to the old days in Hawaii, advocating civil disobedience and violence under their leader, Mano."

Melanie's father commented, "I had heard that, just as I've heard that contemporary political and business leaders take the movement seriously. Do they?"

Mr. Ladd nodded. "Yes. In fact, some high officials have been quoted that an illegal act took place when the Kingdom of Hawaii was overthrown, Queen Lilikuokalani was deposed, and the islands annexed by the United States."

Josh added, "We drove through downtown Honolulu on the one hundredth anniversary of that date. Iolani Palace* was closed and draped in black. The American flag was removed from federal buildings. It was so strange."

His father said, "One man called the state of Hawaii 'our enemy,' and claimed he wanted ku'o ko'a*—that's means "independence" in the Hawaiian language. There's no doubt the kanaka maoli have some serious grievances.

"Native Hawaiians have the shortest life expectancy and the highest mortality rate from stroke, cancer, diabetes, and heart disease. Their mortality rate is ten times higher than any other ethnic group in Hawaii.

"Those who call themselves native Hawaiians represent less than 20 percent of Hawaii's population, yet they account for 70 percent of the prison population. So they naturally feel that the justice system is unfair to them. They have the lowest per capita income, with 80 percent of an estimated 4,000 homeless people living on Hawaii's beaches being native Hawaiians.

"Last, but not least," Mr. Ladd concluded, "the native Hawaiians own less than 1 percent of all businesses. But that's understandable because part of the basic native culture is that they share everything."

"You carry that kind of material in your tourist publication?" Redcliff asked.

"No, because we don't want to upset the six million annual visitors—we never call them tourists—to Hawaii who spend about nine billion dollars. The main thing is that we want this whole thing to be resolved to everyone's satisfaction, without violence."

"Violence is exactly what the Pono Paha faction plans," Redcliff said grimly. "Mano has plans to make your tourists—I mean, visitors—learn this. That's the story I was working on when this message came to our hotel to meet tonight. Mano not only plans to scare them off, but most of us who are non-natives."

"How's he going to do that?" Josh asked as the cab stopped in front of Redcliff's Waikiki hotel.

"Tell you inside," Redcliff replied.

Josh always enjoyed walking through Waikiki's hotel lobbies. Many, like the one where the Redcliffs were staying, were open on all sides except the one where the rooms were. Redcliff led the way toward the elevators, pushing through the inevitable group of Japanese tourists with their cameras.

As Melanie caught a glimpse of herself in the mirrors between the elevators, she squealed. "Oh, Daddy! I look a fright! Why didn't you tell me?"

He chuckled. "I had more important things on my mind than worrying about how the rain messed up your hair."

Josh said impulsively, "You look okay, Melanie."

"Oh, no I don't!" she cried, turning away.

Tank gave Josh a surprised look as they entered the elevator with several Japanese, who chatted away in their own language. Neither Josh nor his companions said anything until they reached Redcliff's and Melanie's adjacent rooms. She excused herself to change clothes.

"Now," Mr. Ladd prompted as Redcliff handed them all towels to dry off, "what did you mean about Pono Paha scaring everybody off these islands?"

Redcliff made sure the door was locked before answering.

"In the course of my investigation, I happened to be in the police station a couple of days when I overheard some plainclothes officers talking about a threat from Mano of the Pono Paha. They're threatening to set off some bombs at the major airports."

"They're what?" Mr. Ladd asked in surprise.

"It's true. I heard the officers saying that Mano figures this will get worldwide press attention. The very threat will keep visitors away in droves. But that's just a start.

"After that, bombs or threats will be used to drive non-locals away, including all of us. Of course, the police are keeping a tight lid on that threat. They don't want to cause a panic while they try to apprehend this Mano and his Pono Paha followers."

Mr. Ladd said soberly, "This Mano is very mysterious because he's never been photographed, he's never held a press conference, and nobody knows where he and his radicals have their headquarters."

Later, Josh, his father, and Tank started to leave just as Melanie reappeared in dry clothes with her hair combed.

Redcliff said, "John, I'm sorry you and the boys are involved in my situation, especially from just trying to do a good deed like helping Melanie and me."

"It's okay, Brad," Mr. Ladd assured him. "The Bible says something about not withholding your hand when it's within your power to do good."

"Well, I don't know much about that, but you certainly did good in keeping Melanie and me from being swept out to sea and drowned!" Redcliff said heartily.

"So," Josh's father added, "since the boys and I did what we should have, I'm confident the good Lord will take care of us."

Josh hoped that was so, but he was still uneasy when the fathers admonished Josh, Tank, and Melanie not to talk about the bomb threat. Everyone said goodnight.

Josh looked at Melanie and said, "I'll call you in the morning." Instantly, he regretted that, for she seemed surprised, and Tank glared at him.

In the hallway leading to the elevators, Tank asked, "Josh, why did you say you'd call her in the morning?"

Josh fumbled for an answer. "Uh . . . she's been through a lot. I was just trying to make her feel better."

"After what she did to you?" Tank demanded. "I hope we never see her again!"

Mr. Ladd hired a taxi for the short ride to the side of Diamond Head,* where both the Ladds and Catletts lived in an apartment building on a deadend street. Josh rode in silence, anguishing over his feelings about Melanie.

While Josh's father paid the taxi driver, Josh and Tank said goodnight. Tank entered his first-floor apartment.

Josh and his dad climbed to the second-floor apartment where they lived. They kicked off their shoes and left them outside the door. This was an Oriental custom they'd learned from other families who resided in the three-story building.

Josh's mother, older sister Tiffany, and younger brother Nathan anxiously waited up for them. While his father explained some of what had happened, Josh excused himself to get out of his wet clothes.

When the lights were finally turned out and Nathan was asleep, Josh lay awake in his twin bed, wondering about the two men, Opu Nui and Holo. Did they really pose a threat to him and his father?

Every time Josh heard a car pull into the driveway behind the apartment, he slipped out of bed and peered out the window. Each time, he breathed a sigh of relief and returned to bed, where he finally slept.

He was awakened by his father standing over his bed. From the look on his face, Josh knew that something was wrong. He sat up quickly, aware that he'd slept late, for the sun was up.

"What is it, Dad?" he asked fearfully.

"Brad just called. Melanie has disappeared."

Chapter Four

THE PONO PAHA STRIKES

Melanie's disappeared?" Josh repeated, sitting bolt upright and throwing off the top sheet. "When? How?"

"Just about an hour ago, on the Windward Side. Brad said he had booked an afternoon flight to the Mainland for Melanie. Because she hadn't had a chance to really see Oahu,* they took an early morning tour bus from the hotel to go around the island. That would have given them time to get back before Melanie's plane left."

Josh jumped out of bed in his shorty pajamas. "Yes? Yes?" His voice betrayed the concern he felt for the girl whom he was sure had cheated him on the Mainland.

"Brad said that when the bus stopped so that people could get out and take pictures, Melanie didn't return. Witnesses had seen her walking along the roadside with her camera, but nobody had seen her disappear. A search turned up no sign of her."

"Those men—Opu and Holo—must have grabbed her, Dad." Josh slipped out of his pajamas and felt in his closet for faded blue jean cutoffs and an old red and yellow flowered aloha* shirt.

"I'm afraid so," Mr. Ladd agreed. "I told Brad we'd be there as soon as I can get a rental car brought around because mine's still on the North Shore."

"Where is Mr. Redcliff now?" Josh asked, sitting on the edge of the bed and pulling on his cutoffs.

"At the police station in Kaneohe."

"Tell me everything else while I finish dressing," Josh urged.

By the time Josh had run a comb through his wavy brown hair and hurriedly brushed his teeth, he knew as much about the situation as his father did. Barefooted as usual, Josh dashed down the hallway saying he had to tell Tank.

At the Catlett's first-floor apartment which faced Diamond Head, Josh started to blurt out what his father had told him. Then he stopped, looking closely at his friend. "What's the matter with you?"

Tank replied in a nasal tone, "Mom says I'm catching cold from being wet so long last night."

Josh didn't believe that being wet in Hawaii's warm December weather could give a person a cold, but he didn't want to argue the point. Instead, he said, "I'm sorry," and then briefly told about Melanie's disappearance.

Tank frowned thoughtfully when Josh had finished. "I don't wish anything bad on anybody, not even Melanie, although she is a royal pain."

"Will you come help look for her?"

Tank shook his head. "I can't. Mom says I've got to stay quiet until she sees if this really is a cold."

"Maybe it's only an allergy," Josh said hopefully.

"Whatever it is, I feel lousy."

Through the open screen door, Josh heard his mother calling. He stepped outside and looked up. Mrs. Ladd leaned over the railing on the second story directly overhead. "Josh, I need some bread and milk before the rental car arrives and you and your father have to go. Please run down to the little store right away."

"Ah, Mom! Why can't Nathan do it?"

"He's playing over at his friend's house. Tiffany's visiting her girlfriend down the street. Here, catch this." She dropped a five-dollar bill.

Josh caught the fluttering currency, said goodbye to Tank, and hurried down the one-way street. The usual mynah* birds hopped out of the way, but Josh barely noticed. His thoughts raced.

Those two men have grabbed Melanie. What'll they do to her? Will they come after Tank and me next?

Josh reached the little store on the through street that T'd off of the apartment's one-way drive. He made the purchases and started back toward home, deep in thought. He was passing some be-still trees* on the left side of the roadway when he heard a car behind him.

He looked back, and his heart jumped at sight of a black sedan. *It's them!* his mind screamed. *The same two men who beat up on Melanie's father and threatened her!*

Josh debated whether to run or continue walking casually. *They didn't get a good look at me last night,* he reminded himself, aware that his heart had speeded up. *I'll just act natural. Besides, they wouldn't dare do anything to me in broad daylight—would they?*

While he debated that idea, the car pulled up alongside him and stopped. "Hey, kid!" A man called.

Josh was tempted to break into a wild run toward home, but instead, he forced himself to turn and calmly face the haole driver. "Yes?" he asked, feeling great relief that it wasn't either of the two men from last night.

"I'm looking for a guy named Frank Mitsu who's supposed to live around here. You know him?"

"Sorry," Josh said, glad his heartbeat was slowing. "I don't know the name."

The man thanked him and drove slowly on to stop by a group of younger boys trying to remove a coconut husk with a long metal spike upended in a two-by-four.

"Whew!" Josh breathed, continuing his walk. "I'm sure jumpy! I thought that . . . Oh-Oh!"

His intensely blue eyes probed ahead to where the be-still trees ended and a clump of tall bamboo grew beside a hole in a chain-link fence.

Kamuela Kong stepped through the bamboo with a scowl on his huge brown face. "King" Kong, a name nobody dared call him to his face, was only 13, but he stood almost six feet tall and weighed around 200 pounds. If he'd worn shoes, they would have been size 13 quadruple E.

Barefooted as always, he wore only a pair of old khaki pants cut off at the knees and a tattered green and yellow aloha shirt. Kong growled deep in his throat, like an animal, glaring at Josh with deep brown eyes. Wide, flaring nostrils above large, thick lips warned Josh that the neighborhood bully was happy at catching a victim alone. Kong had only one real friend, his younger sister. Kanani* was totally unlike him, yet everyone knew Kong was very fond of her.

"Hi, Kong." Josh tried to keep his voice from quivering. "How're you doing?"

"You get stink ear,"* he said in pidgin* English.

"I listen just fine," Josh protested, shifting the bag of bread and milk so he could drop them in a hurry and try to defend himself if necessary.

The big kid shook his head of curly brown hair that grew wildly in every direction. "No, you Mainland malihini.* Kong tell you not walk dis way." He waved a brown-skinned hand the size of a ripe coconut. "Dis belong me, Kong. No haole boy walk heah."

Josh licked his lips nervously, knowing that an encounter with King Kong always ended the same. "There's no other way to our apartment except along here," Josh explained reasonably. "My mother needed some bread and milk, so I went..."

"Soon you haoles all leave dis place, go back to da Mainland. Leave dese islands to us kanaka maoli. Mano of the Pono Paha say so!"

In spite of the immediate concern for his health, Josh

pounced on the name of the radical leader. "You ever meet this Mano in person?" Josh asked, hoping the question would divert Kong until Josh could find a way out of his predicament.

Kong swelled his great chest importantly. "Me, Kong, goin' be da kine* Pono Paha Young Warrior!"

Josh had heard that the radical leader had a recruitment movement along Hawaii's youth, but he wasn't sure whether it was true or just another of the many rumors floating around the islands.

"You are?" Josh asked. "When?"

"Saturday morning!" Kong thumped his massive chest with a big hand. "Fly me to meeting at Kapu Falls!* Mano hisself make me member! Someday we drive all da kine haoles from dis land! Be like before when King Kamehameha* lead warriors in battle. No moh haole kakaroach.*"

Josh frowned, trying to remember the meaning of the last pidgin word. It wasn't what it sounded like, but something else. *Oh yes! Theft or ripoff!*

"Why do you hate us haoles?" Josh asked the question that had troubled him since he'd first literally bumped into Kong and earned his lasting hatred.

"Not only haoles!" Kong waved his hands to take in the whole island. "All not born dis place. Only kanaka maoli stay when Pono Paha done!"

"But you're only part Hawaiian." Josh wasn't sure he should have said that, but it had slipped out as another logical statement.

"Most Hawaiians live dis place hapa,* like me," Kong agreed. "But we real kamaaina.* Stay dis place when all haole gone. Mano say so."

Josh realized that Kong was dead serious, and apparently so was the mysterious leader of the radical Pono Paha movement.

"We've all lived together for a long time in these islands," he pointed out. "Everybody talks about the aloha spirit. So it's not logical that it'll go back to the way it was, although everybody seems to agree that native Hawaiians have suffered some wrongs that need to be righted. So for now, let's get along together."

"You call Kong liar?"

"No! Of course not!" Josh said hastily, but he realized it was too late.

Anger twisted Kong's face as he exclaimed, "You lolo* malihini. We pau* talk. Now Kong break you' face!"

"Hey! I didn't mean . . ." He let his voice trail off as Kong reached into his back pocket and pulled out a pair of thin, black leather gloves. Josh gulped audibly, knowing what that meant.

Neighborhood kids had told Josh that Kong had long ago seen an old movie where the gunman always pulled on black leather gloves before drawing on some helpless sodbuster.* This action added to the victim's fear.

Kong certainly increased Josh's anxiety by the slow, deliberate act of drawing on each glove, then flexing the fingers before curling them into anvil-hard fists.

Josh swallowed hard, but the lump in his throat wouldn't go down. Josh debated whether to try defending himself or run like a scared mongoose.*

As Kong cocked his right fist with the sun glistening on the shiny black leather glove, Josh was aware of cars stopping behind him. He didn't dare take his eyes off of Kong until he lowered his fist and looked beyond Josh.

"Say, boys," the first driver called, "I'm supposed to deliver this rental to somebody named Ladd. Do either of you know which apartment he lives in?"

Josh let out a glad cry and whirled around. A white four-door sedan was driven by a young man who had spoken. The second car, stopped behind the sedan, was green and white with a large sign on the front door panel, *Rent-A-Car. We deliver.*

Josh exclaimed, "I'm his son, so I'll show you." He raced around the front of the first vehicle and slid into the front seat before Kong could react. As the driver put the car into gear, Kong yelled and shook a black-gloved fist, but Josh didn't care. He turned to the driver. "We live in the second apartment building."

When Josh's father had signed the car rental agreement papers, the young driver left in the second vehicle. Josh and his father said goodbye to Mrs. Ladd and headed inland to pick up the Lunalilo* Freeway. They switched to the Likelike* Highway and climbed up the Koolau Range to pass through the Wilson Tunnel into Kaneohe.

They found Melanie's distraught father waiting outside

the police station. He stuck his head through the driver's side window and shook hands with Mr. Ladd.

"Thanks for coming," Redcliff said in an emotional voice. "I've been going out of my mind."

Josh opened the front door. "Where did it happen?" he asked, sliding into the back seat so both men could sit up front.

"We were up by Punaluu.* You know the area?"

Josh and his father nodded. "I know," Mr. Ladd said. "Shall we start from there? You can tell us the rest of the details on the way."

"I told you on the phone what little I know." Redcliff slammed his open palm on the dashboard. "It's my fault! I should never have let her out of my sight! But with a busload of people along, I never dreamed she'd be in any danger."

"What do the police say?" Josh asked, feeling some of the anguish Melanie's father was suffering.

"At first, they were inclined to treat it as a missing person case instead of a possible kidnapping. When I explained what had happened last night, they changed their minds. But the FBI isn't usually called in on a case until 48 hours have passed."

"You mean, nobody's looking for her?" Josh asked in surprise as his father headed toward Kamehameha Highway* which runs along the northeastern shore of the island.

"Oh, they're looking, but naturally nobody's going to look as hard as I am—I mean, as we will."

Josh wanted to ask what Mr. Redcliff thought would happen to Melanie, but decided it wasn't a good question. So he kept quiet as they followed along the shoreline until they came to where Melanie had vanished.

Josh and the two men got out. Behind them, the mountains rose steeply into the air for a thousand feet. Before them, beyond a white sand beach, the Pacific Ocean stretched toward the horizon. It was a beautiful, peaceful spot, but Josh felt no peace inside.

"The bus was parked there," Redcliff said, pointing. "The passengers spread out in both directions to take pictures or walk along the beach. I stopped to talk to the driver, as I often do. As a writer, I sometimes learn things that way. Melanie took her camera and wandered off down that way with some of the others."

Josh turned to follow the man's finger back the way they'd come. Some palm trees swayed in the wind, their fronds making loud rattling sounds. "Didn't the people she was with see what happened to her?"

Redcliff shook his head. "They said she was scrambling down onto the beach, wanting to take a close-up of something with her camera."

Josh hesitated, then asked, "Is there any chance that she went into the ocean?"

Redcliff shook his head. "I'm sure she didn't drown. Even if she fell in, she's a strong swimmer. So I'm positive those men abducted her."

Melanie's father sighed, then added, "I didn't realize she was missing until we all got back on the bus. The driver let me out again. I ran back and checked, but . . ." His voice cracked, and he lowered his head.

Josh fought down his own emotions, which surged like the sea. His father walked over and clapped a comforting hand on Redcliff's shoulder. Josh turned away, then slowly made his way back along the highway. Occasional cars passed, but it was generally quiet. Josh wanted it that way, to be alone with his thoughts.

Josh glanced out to where the whitecaps broke into fine spray. *She did me wrong, over and over. So why should I feel so concerned?*

He pursed his lips. *Maybe it's because it's the Christian thing to do,* he decided.

He paused for one last look around, then slowly turned and headed back toward the two men. His bare toe struck something, sending it skittering onto the highway.

Absently, he bent and picked it up. Then he blinked and looked again.

That's her pin! The one that should have been mine! He picked it up and starting running back toward the car. "Dad! Mr. Redcliff! Look what I found!"

But Josh realized he had found something else too. He knew why he cared. *We've got to find her!* he told himself, adding firmly, *And we will! Or I will!*

Instantly, he wondered, *What am I getting myself into?* But he really didn't want to know, for the thought scared him plenty.

Chapter Five

DEMONSTRATION OF POWER

The men decided to return to Honolulu where Redcliff said detectives would contact him at his hotel.

As Mr. Ladd turned the rental car around, he said, "Maybe they'll now have more information about Melanie's kidnapping. I would think they have already interviewed the bus driver and the passengers in hopes one of them saw something that'll help find her."

In the back seat, Josh thoughtfully studied the pin that Melanie had dropped. It was a simple, round, gold-colored emblem consisting of the traditional lighted lamp which represented learning, with the words, "Top Scholarship Honors, Valley Elementary School." Yet to Josh it was much more than a pin.

He released the safety clasp and ran the pin through his shirt. *That's where it belongs,* he told himself. But he didn't feel right about that. *It was given to Melanie, even if she did cheat me out of it. But now she's missing.* He removed the pin and carefully slipped it into his pocket.

"Something's been bothering me, Mr. Redcliff," he said, leaning forward and resting his elbows on the back of the front seat. "If the Pono Paha people are mad at you, why didn't they kidnap you instead of Melanie?"

Her father turned around to look at Josh with sad eyes. "I suspect they knew that there's no greater pain to a parent than to have a child in jeopardy. They must believe that I'll do anything to get her back safely, like not writing about Mano or the Pono Paha."

Mr. Ladd observed, "That's certainly possible, but I don't see how your magazine story, no matter how good it is, could really make a difference to the Pono Paha."

"You think it's something else, John?"

"I hope I'm wrong, Brad, but I've got a hunch Melanie is more than just a kidnap victim."

Josh was intrigued. "Such as?" he prompted.

"I don't know, son. But in light of all the things going on about the sovereignty movement, I think this abduction might well be something else."

Back in Honolulu, they parked in the underground garage and took the elevator up to the hotel lobby. Josh followed the two men across the open area filled with antherium,* orchids, birds-of-paradise, and other Hawaiian flowers. From beyond the open expanse of lobby, past the large wicker and rattan chairs and sofas, Josh saw people happily swimming in the clear blue pool. Nobody seemed to have any cares.

At the desk, Redcliff asked the pretty brown-skinned clerk in her colorful muumuu* if there were any messages for him. She checked, then handed him an envelope. Melanie's father ripped it open, dropped the envelope, and silently read the enclosed sheet of paper. Josh picked up the envelope and stuck it in his back pocket.

With a strangled cry, Redcliff sagged into a high-backed wicker chair. The paper slipped from his fingers.

Josh's father retrieved the note. Josh stepped close and read the typed words.

Your daughter will be sacrificed Saturday noon as a warning of what will happen to other invaders unless these islands are promptly cleansed of their presence.

Mr. Ladd handed the paper to Josh, then reached out to comfort Redcliff, who sat in stunned and painful silence. Josh continued reading the message.

All non-Hawaiians must quickly vacate the islands, so they can be restored to their original state. Do not notify the press until after an island-wide demonstration of power which will soon follow the noon deadline. The combined events will prove to all skeptics what will happen to all non-kanaka maoli if these lands are not returned to their rightful owners.

It was signed, *Mano of the Pono Paha.*

Josh exclaimed, "They can't be serious! This is Wednesday, so that's only two-and-a-half days away."

Mr. Ladd stood up from where he was kneeling by Melanie's stricken father, ignoring the stares of people walking by. Mr. Ladd took a couple of steps away as Josh followed. Speaking so softly only Josh could hear, Mr. Ladd said,

"Human sacrifice was a very ancient practice in the islands, but I haven't heard of it being done in many centuries."

Josh thought of the lava heiaus,* a place where Hawaiians had held their sacred rites long before the haoles arrived in the islands. The heiaus, whether in ruins or good condition, were still scattered throughout the islands.

Then Josh flinched as another possible sacrifice site flashed in his mind. Without remembering to whisper, he asked, "Dad, you don't think the note means Pele* and the volcanoes, do you?"

"Pele?" Redcliff cried, leaping up to join Josh and his father. "I know that name! She's the Hawaiian goddess of fire, who lives in the volcanoes. Do you think . . . ?"

Mr. Ladd interrupted quickly, "No, of course not. For one thing, the volcanoes on the Big Island aren't erupting right now."

"But there are still some fire pits," Redcliff said grimly. "Melanie and I walked back to see one. It was like looking into hell itself."

Josh shuddered, remembering when he and his family had also hiked across acres of rough lava to peer down into a pit the length of a football field. Even before they had reached the site, the ground moaned like a monstrous animal in pain. When the choking sulphurous fumes blew away, Josh saw that red-hot lava sloshed back and forth across the bottom, spewing flames up the sides of the pit.

Redcliff pressed both hands to his face in anguish. "No matter what this Mano plans, we can't let them do anything to

Melanie! We have to find her!"

"We will," Josh said, feeling terrible about his thoughtless mention of Pele. To him, Pele was a myth, a legend, but in Hawaii many people still believed in her. Some of Josh's friends at school were firmly convinced that Pele lived. So were many adults, including some haoles, judging from what Josh had seen on television during some of the volcanic eruptions on the Big Island.

Josh had seen people throw offerings to Pele to appease her anger and stop her from pouring lava over their land. These gifts included many items, such as berries that were supposedly sacred to Pele. But of course, there were no human sacrifices.

Josh mused, "I wonder what the note means about an 'island-wide demonstration of power'?"

"The note didn't demand any ransom," Redcliff replied. "The Pono Paha are not bargaining. They snatched Melanie for some other reason than making me stop writing about them, or exchanging her for money. Remember what you said on the way back from the Windward Side, John?" he asked in a low voice. "Maybe you're right; there is something more to this than kidnapping my daughter."

Josh felt a slow, painful tightening of his throat and chest. "You mean, no matter what we do, unless we find her in time, they're going to . . .?" He couldn't finish the sentence, because the thought was so terrible.

His father didn't answer, but shoved the note into his shirt pocket and grabbed Redcliff's arm. "Come on, Brad! Let's call the police."

The trio hurried to a bank of pay phones in the lobby. Melanie's father picked up the receiver, but his hand started shaking so hard he couldn't dial. Mr. Ladd placed the call.

While his father talked with the police, Josh glanced out across the lobby without walls. His gaze swept past the small waterfall to the swimming pool with people sunning in lounge chairs. Josh's eyes flickered to the passage leading to Waikiki's main street.

Pale-skinned Mainland men strolled by. Many wore ridiculous-looking black leather shoes, white socks, new colorful aloha shirts, and shorts that fell to their knobby knees. The women wore lauhala* hats and muumuus.

What demonstration of power could anybody make to stop people from visiting Hawaii? Josh wondered. Then his thoughts jumped to Melanie. He suppressed another shudder at the thought of Mano's terrible threat to her as contained in the note.

Josh asked himself fiercely, *Why don't the police do something? And why are we standing here like this instead of trying to find her?* Then he sighed. *But where do we even start looking for her?*

When Mr. Ladd turned the phone over to Melanie's father, Josh voiced his thoughts to his dad.

Mr. Ladd walked away toward a splashing fountain in the lobby, motioning Josh to follow. "While Brad's on the phone, I want to say something to you."

He glanced around to make sure nobody was near, then

lowered his voice. "Remember what Brad said earlier about something he'd overheard at the police station?"

"You mean about a bomb threat to the airports?"

"Yes. I hope I'm not being an alarmist, but I've thought of something that deeply concerns me."

Josh stirred uneasily. "What's that?"

"I wonder if it's possible that one or more small nuclear bombs could have been stolen or bought from one of those countries that used to be part of the Soviet Union."

Josh's eyes opened wide in fright. "You mean, maybe the Pono Paha . . .?"

"I hope not, but if it happened, everybody would be in danger, and not just Melanie, but her father, and maybe you, Tank, and me."

Josh stared at his father, thinking of the note's ominous words, *an island-wide demonstration of power.*

"Ah, Dad, even the Pono Paha wouldn't dare do that, would they?"

"There are a lot of unscrupulous people in the world, Son. Sometimes it seems that everybody who has any kind of a weapon is willing to sell it to anybody who'll pay the price. Maybe this Pono Paha group is angry enough to have bought or stolen such a terrible bomb."

Josh glanced past the lobby and the swimming pool to Kalakaua Avenue,* Waikiki's main street, which ran within a hundred yards of the ocean. Unconcerned visitors strolled in the warm December sun. Then Josh whirled back to face his father.

"If the Pono Paha gang really does have one of those bombs, they could blow up an airport! That would ruin the tourist business and scare everybody that's here so they'd want to get away. There'd be nobody left!"

"Except those who feel they belong here. You're thinking exactly the same way I am."

The enormity of the possibility staggered Josh. He shook his head vigorously, trying to dislodge the thought that this might be true.

His father reexamined the note. "This was obviously written by someone who's educated," he commented. "I wish we knew more about Mano, their leader."

"He sure hates haoles," Josh said bitterly. "Anybody who would threaten to do such an awful thing to a girl, and to this state . . ."

"Shh! Brad's off the phone."

Father and son hurried to meet Redcliff. He said, "The detectives are on their way. They want to meet me in my room. They'd like you two to be there too."

While waiting for the detectives, Melanie's father anxiously paced the carpeted floor of his hotel room. Mr. Ladd sat at the small writing desk, thoughtfully studying the Pono Paha note. Josh stood at the window facing the Koolaus.* Deep in thought, he barely noticed the magnificent white clouds sailing majestically over the green mountain range.

Melanie's father exclaimed, "John, I'm going out of my mind! Help me think!"

"I'm trying, Brad. I've been wondering about some things in this note. For example, when we think of Pele, we automatically think of the Big Island, because that's where the only active volcanoes are."

"So?" Redcliff asked shortly.

Josh turned around to look at his father, who got up from the desk and faced Redcliff. "So I wonder if that means the kidnappers have already taken Melanie to the Big Island?" Mr. Ladd mused. "Or is that simply a ruse, a trick to throw us off the track? Could she still be here on Oahu, or even on another island?"

Redcliff said thoughtfully. "I don't know, but her abductors could have flown Melanie to any island in a private plane. It'd be too risky for them to take a commercial inter-island jet. Somebody might remember them."

Sitting down at the desk where his father had been before, Josh said, "But Hawaii is such a big island we'd never find Melanie without some hint as to where to start looking. That's true even if the note is a trick and she's been taken to one of the other islands."

"Well," Mr. Ladd said with a heavy sigh, "there's one thing for sure. We're now in a race against time: Saturday noon, two-and-a-half days from now." He added, "But we'll find her, Brad. We'll find her in time."

"How?" Redcliff almost roared in his anguish. "We don't have a single, solid clue as to where to start looking for her! Not one."

Josh squirmed uncomfortably at something in his pocket.

Absently, he pulled out the envelope in which the note had been delivered. He fingered it thoughtfully and turned it over. Suddenly, he looked down. His fingers had touched some indentations below the flap. Josh held the envelope closer.

"There's something here," he announced, tilting the envelope so the light hit it better. "Looks as if someone had written on a piece of paper laid over the envelope and made an impression. See, Dad?"

His father took the envelope and studied it. He picked up a pencil from beside the phone pad and lightly stroked over the indentations.

Josh leaned closer as the flying pencil point revealed two words. "Forbidden Falls," he read aloud.

Melanie's father took the envelope and stared at the two words. "That looks like Melanie's handwriting."

"You sure?" Mr. Ladd asked.

"No, but it sure looks like it. Maybe she's trying to let us know where she is."

Mr. Ladd said, "I've never heard of that place. Have you?"

When Redcliff shook his head, Mr. Ladd said, "There's a Sacred Falls on Oahu not far from where we were at Punaluu. But that's not a likely place for the Pono Paha. They'd have a remote area in which to hide."

Josh exclaimed, "I'll call the front desk for a map. Maybe we've got our first break!"

Chapter Six

IN SEARCH OF
FORBIDDEN FALLS

Josh didn't wait for a bellman to bring the map, but raced
out of the hotel room to the elevators. On the way, Josh
felt his spirits lift.

*Melanie must have had a moment alone to make that note
on the envelope before the kidnappers had it delivered,* he
told himself. *She used her head on that. Maybe now we've
got a chance to find her before Saturday noon. But where is
Forbidden Falls?*

In the lobby he dashed through another group of Japanese
visitors and stopped breathlessly at the bellman's desk. Josh
didn't think of tipping, but took the map, said "Thanks!" and
headed back upstairs.

He joined his father and Redcliff in examining the state
map. Josh's hopes began to sag as they scanned each of the
seven main islands.

"There are waterfalls everywhere!" he exclaimed after
awhile. "There's Akaka Falls* and Waipio Falls* plus others
on the Big Island, and at least a dozen on Kauai!* The tallest

55

one is on Maui.* But we haven't found one that's called Forbidden Falls. So we're right back where we started—nowhere!"

Shaking his head, Mr. Ladd commented, "Maybe not. Waipio Falls is up here toward the northeast tip of the Big Island." He put his finger on the map. "Waipio Valley* is very remote and mostly uninhabited. There's a lot of ancient Hawaiian history connected with that area."

Melanie's father said, "I'm not familiar with this state's history. What's so important about that area?"

Mr. Ladd explained, "The great King Kamehameha, who conquered and unified these islands long ago, was born at the northeast tip of the Big Island and was schooled at nearby Waipio Valley."

"We've been there," Josh said. "You have to hike or take a four-wheel-drive vehicle. The valley is only about nine miles long, and it gets narrower and narrower as you get toward the back."

"That's right, son. The entrance to the ancient Hawaiian underworld was supposed to be there."

"It was?" Melanie's father asked. When Mr. Ladd nodded, Redcliff added soberly. "It makes sense that the Pono Paha people would take Melanie there." He again glanced at the map. "That's not far from the volcanoes."

Josh said, "But there are no Forbidden Falls there."

"Maybe the Hawaiians call them something else," his father replied as someone knocked at the door.

"That'll be the detectives," Redcliff said, hurrying to

admit them. "Now maybe we'll get somewhere."

Half an hour later, Josh took a deep breath and let it out slowly. Ted Pims, a haole plainclothesman, looked like a football linebacker with massive shoulders on a big frame. His partner, Curtis Chow, was a trim, slightly built man of Chinese descent whose loose-fitting aloha shirt couldn't hide his well-developed biceps.

The officers had completed their interrogation and taken possession of the warning note and envelope with its intriguing two-word message.

"We understand your concern, Mr. Redcliff," Chow assured him, "but we suggest that you and your friends let law-enforcement officers handle this."

"I can't just sit here and do nothing!" Melanie's father cried in exasperation. "You read that warning! We only have until Saturday noon. That's just two-and-a-half days away."

"Take it easy," the haole detective advised. "There are elements of this case that you don't know about. If you try to help, no matter how good your intentions, you may do a whole lot more harm than good."

Josh glanced at his father and saw that he was thinking the same thing. *A bomb! Maybe the rumor about the nuclear bomb is true. But even if it's only a regular bomb, that would be terrible enough.*

Melanie's father protested vigorously, but the plainclothesmen were firm. With another warning to stay out of the investigation and a promise to do what they could to find Melanie, they left.

Josh felt sorry for the girl's father. His face was pale and drawn. "What am I going to do, John?" he cried on an anguished note. "I can't just wait around, doing nothing, while time runs out on my daughter's life!"

"Let's take a drive back to where those men attacked you and look around," Mr. Ladd suggested. "That shouldn't interfere with the police investigation. While we drive, I'm sure we can think of something to help Melanie."

That was agreeable to her father, so Mr. Ladd called his wife to report the plan. She said Tank had been waiting for Josh to come home. Tank wanted to talk to Josh for a moment. When he got on the line, he said his mother had taken him to the doctor. He diagnosed an allergy and ordered a prescription. Tank said he felt fine and wanted permission to ride along.

Josh asked his father, who checked with Redcliff. He was impatient to get started, but he was agreeable to stopping for Tank because he wasn't out of the way.

In the back seat on the short ride from the Waikiki hotel to the apartments, Josh listened to the two men in the front seat. They discussed ways to find Melanie without interfering with the authorities' investigation.

"I've got a friend, Olin Palmer, who lives in Waimea,* on the Big Island," Mr. Ladd said. "That's not far from the Waipio area. Olin has lived in the islands for many years. He married a local girl whose father was a kahuna,* or priest. Olin might be able to help us."

"Let's phone him," Redcliff said.

"He doesn't have a phone. He lives rather simply on a rural road. He doesn't like his peace and serenity disrupted by jangling telephones. We'd have to fly to the Big Island, then drive inland to see him. Of course, it could be a wild goose chase, and he may not be able to help us."

"I'll think about it," Melanie's father said.

Josh was really pleased when his best friend slid into the back seat with him a few minutes later. Josh quickly and quietly brought Tank up to date on everything.

"Where are we going?" Josh asked as the car cruised along H1, the Lunalilo Freeway.

"First," his father answered. "We'll drive through one of those fast-food places and pick up something to eat while we drive. Then we'll go to where Brad's house washed into the sea. Maybe we can find some car tracks or something that'll give us a clue toward getting Melanie back. On the return trip, I'll stop at the garage where my station wagon was towed and see if it's ready."

"By then," Redcliff said, "we'll have decided whether to risk flying to the Big Island to see if John's friend can help us."

As the car passed Punchbowl,* a long-extinct volcano known officially as the National Memorial Cemetery of the Pacific, Josh wondered about Melanie. *How can we possibly find her before Saturday?*

Tank seemed to be thinking the same thing. He leaned close to Josh and said in a low voice, "There's so little time left, and we're just driving around in hopes of finding some clue or something to help here."

Josh observed, "I thought you didn't like Melanie?"

"I didn't say I did. I just wouldn't like anyone to end up in a volcano."

"The note didn't say a volcano," Josh reminded him. "The Pono Paha could be planning to use a heiau."

"Those are everywhere!" Tank swept his arms wide. "At least, their ruins are all over these islands. We'd never find the right one out of so many."

"I know. I was just trying to think of something besides the volcanoes. We need to find those Forbidden Falls."

"Well, wherever she is, I don't think there's a thing we can do to help her before it's too late."

"There you go—looking at the dark side of things again."

"I'm just being practical," Tank insisted.

Josh reached into his pocket and pulled out the scholarship pin. He opened the clasp and slid the pin into his shirt.

"Why're you doing that?" Tank asked.

Josh wasn't really sure, so he shrugged. "Oh, sort of putting something where I can see it and think about Melanie wearing it again."

"She has no right to wear that, and you know it!"

"Just the same, I'm going to give it back to her when she's found."

"*If* she's found."

"We'll find her," Josh said firmly, then lapsed into silence as his father pulled off the freeway, heading for a restaurant. *I pray we find her,* Josh told himself, but inside, he had grave doubts.

They ate in the car, driving inland past pineapple and sugarcane fields toward the ocean. Then they swung to the right and followed the North Shore. Josh glanced out to sea. "Wow!" he exclaimed. "Those big waves are still coming in!"

"Forty feet high, I'll bet," Tank said with awe. "Look at them!"

Josh stared in wonder as the mountainous waves closed in all along the horizon. He rolled down his window to watch the waves start to fold over on themselves, then collapse. Seconds later, the sound reached him. "Craaack!" The air seemed to reverberate with the power of the waves.

"It's coming from all directions!" Tank cried. "I wonder if you and I'll ever be good enough to surf really big waves?"

"I'm satisfied to watch the experts ride the Banzai Pipeline,"* Josh said firmly. He leaned forward to ask, "Dad, do you think there's any danger of those waves crossing the road and catching us as they did before?"

"The authorities haven't closed the road, so I'm sure it's safe."

Josh wasn't quite so sure, but he sat back and watched the incredible display of power from the ocean until they neared the site of their wild experience of the night before last.

Everyone lapsed into silence as the car moved smoothly along the highway. *I want some action,* Josh thought. *But I'm sure Melanie's father wants it even more than I do.*

Josh's eyes flickered to Mr. Redcliff, who was also watching the ocean's huge waves. Josh's glance moved on to the right, seeing a few houses standing on a small rise beyond the reach of the threatening sea.

As they started to pass a side road on the right, Josh suddenly stiffened and stared. "Dad!" he cried, reaching forward to grip his father by the right shoulder. "There's their car again!"

"Whose car?" Mr. Ladd asked, looking around. "Oh!" he exclaimed, understanding. "You're right! It's that same black sedan."

"But where are the men?" Josh asked. "Opu Nui and Holo?"

His eyes darted ahead to where the house had stood before sliding into the ocean. "There they are!"

The other three in the car followed Josh's hand pointing through the windshield.

"Why're they walking backwards?" Tank asked.

"They're raking the driveway!" Mr. Ladd exclaimed. "Getting rid of the tracks their car left so the police can't make molds or take pictures of them. At the same time, they're wiping out their own footprints. When they get back to the roadway, they'll walk on the pavement back to their car because their tracks won't show."

"Don't slow down!" Redcliff warned as Josh's father eased off on the accelerator. "They'll get suspicious! Just keep going! And don't look at them!"

"They can't recognize us," Tank replied as the car passed the two men with rakes. "They didn't get a good look at us last night."

"No, but they could recognize me!" Mr. Redcliff

answered, swiveling his face sharply away toward the ocean. He also slid down into the seat as the car drew even with Opu Nui and Holo.

Josh forced his gaze away from them, but tried to see them out of the corner of his eye. He saw the one with the big stomach glance up and stop raking.

"Oh-oh!" Josh said under his breath. "Opu Nui is looking at us!"

As the car moved steadily on, Redcliff asked, "John, do you think they could have recognized me before I turned my head?"

Mr. Ladd warned, "Boys, don't look back." He glanced in the rearview mirror. "I don't think so, Brad. Those men are still raking, so they didn't recognize you."

"Dad," Josh said, "Could we turn around and follow them when they leave? They might lead us to . . ."

"Good idea!" Melanie's father broke in. "Pull over as soon as you can, John. Park where we can see them when they leave."

Mr. Ladd found another driveway and turned around. Then he pulled beside some oleanders growing along the roadside and parked.

"We can see them from here," he explained. "But I hope they can't see us. Now, we wait."

It seemed to Josh that it took a long time for the men to finish their work, but they finally backed onto the paved highway. They shouldered their rakes and headed back toward their car.

"Get ready, John," Redcliff urged.

Josh kept his eye on the two Pono Paha members as his father turned the key in the ignition. When the Pono Paha members pulled into the highway and turned left, Mr. Ladd eased his rental car onto the pavement.

"Stay well back, John," Redcliff advised, "but don't lose them."

"I'll do my best, Brad."

Two other cars passed. Mr. Ladd said that was good. Having a couple of other cars between them would keep the men in the black car from getting suspicious.

Josh eagerly leaned forward with Tank, anxiously observing the black sedan as it moved down Highway 83, passed Haleiwa, and turned onto Highway 99, commonly called the Kam Highway instead of Kamehameha. Traffic was heavier here.

"Looks as if they're heading for Honolulu," Tank commented. "We'll never be able to follow them if they get in that traffic."

"Let's just hope they don't notice us staying behind them all this distance," Mr. Ladd answered. "If they do, there's no telling what they might try."

Josh was glad something was happening, even if he wasn't sure that following the suspect car would lead them to Melanie. When the black sedan took H1 near Pearl City, mingling with still more traffic, Josh tapped his dad on the shoulder.

"What if they're heading for the airport? We're getting near it."

"About all we could do is try to hang back and do our best to keep them in sight, Son. If they go to a ticket window or gate, we'll try to find out their destination. Hey! Where'd they go?"

Josh joined the others in studying the steady stream of traffic, but there was no sign of the black sedan.

"That's strange," Josh commented, turning to look in the lanes beside their car, then behind it.

Suddenly Josh cried, "Dad! They're right behind us, and coming up fast!"

Chapter Seven

A BOMB SCARE

Josh added in an excited tone, "I think they're going to ram us!" He automatically tensed himself for the expected rear-end crash.

"I don't think they'd risk doing that on a busy highway like this," his father replied, speeding up. "They don't know who we are, but they probably became suspicious of us staying behind them so long. Maybe they dropped back in another lane to get a better look at us. Brad, be ready to look away from them when they pass."

Josh glanced at Tank, who gripped the back of the front seat and braced himself. Josh's eyes moved to his father. He was watching the rearview mirror.

"Well, would you look at that!" he exclaimed. "An officer in an unmarked car has turned on his red light behind the black sedan."

Josh swiveled his head to see that it was true. Hawaii has no highway patrol, so police in both marked and unmarked cars do all the traffic enforcement in both city and rural areas. Josh sighed with relief as the black sedan slowed and pulled off the highway.

Mr. Ladd slowed. "Traffic's pretty heavy, but if I can find a place to pull off, I'd like to talk to that officer. He's probably giving the driver a ticket for following us too closely."

By the time Josh's father could find another place to stop, the officer and the black sedan were a good quarter mile behind. "Can't back up that far," Mr. Ladd announced, "and it's too dangerous walk back in this heavy traffic. We'll just have to go on."

Redcliff commented in a discouraged tone, "There goes our chance of following those two men and maybe finding Melanie."

"Not necessarily, Brad. The officer will have the driver's name and address on the ticket. They won't give us that information, but it will be available to those detectives, Chow and Pim."

Josh suggested, "Let's find a phone and call them."

Mr. Ladd said, "That information won't be available until the officer comes in at the end of his shift."

"But this is an emergency," Josh reminded them. "The police cars all have radios, so maybe the detectives could contact that officer back there right away."

Mr. Ladd agreed that was possible, and took the first off-ramp where a service station was visible. There he found a phone booth and made his call.

Josh anxiously waited outside the booth with Tank and Melanie's father until Mr. Ladd hung up.

"I reached Detective Chow. But the problem is I couldn't

tell him anything specific except the approximate time and location of the stop, that the officer drove an unmarked car, and stopped a black sedan with two male occupants."

"You mean he can't help us?" Melanie's father asked with a crestfallen look.

"Oh, Chow's going to try. I'm to call him back in 20 minutes. Meantime, I'm going to call the garage and see how they're doing with my station wagon."

While his father made the second call, Josh and Tank paced around the service station's paved area, watching cars come and go. Melanie's father stood apart, staring toward the intensely green mountains with the puffy white clouds soaring above them.

"I feel so sorry for him," Tank said in his slow, easygoing manner. "Every minute counts, and he's forced to stand here and wait, doing nothing."

"I'm sort of tense inside, myself," Josh admitted, fingering the scholarship pin on his shirt.

"Maybe the detectives will have something when your dad calls back," Tank said as Mr. Ladd hung up the phone and stepped out of the booth.

"The garage man said that my station wagon won't be ready before tomorrow," he explained with a touch of exasperation in his voice.

"Never mind about that," Redcliff said crisply. "Call that detective back and see what he learned about the men in that black sedan."

Mr. Ladd consulted his wrist watch. "It isn't time yet.

Sergeant Chow told me 20 minutes."

"Call him anyway," Melanie's father said a little sharply. "I can't stand around here like this, knowing my daughter's life is in danger."

Josh glanced at Tank, who lowered his voice. "He's getting kind of touchy, huh?"

"I can't blame him," Josh whispered back, watching his father return to the phone booth.

When he returned this time, Mr. Ladd took a deep breath and blew it out noisily. "Mr. Chow was polite, but I could sense some irritation in his tone. He hasn't been able to find out anything yet."

Mr. Redcliff snapped, "I wish those cops hurt as I do! Then they'd move faster."

Josh's father said soothingly, "I'm sure they're doing the best they can, Brad."

"Well, it's not good enough!"

Josh exchanged looks with Tank, who muttered, "He shouldn't be taking his anger out on your dad."

As Josh nodded, Mr. Ladd said quietly, "There's one more thing, Brad."

"What's that?" he growled.

"Chow again said for us to stay out of this investigation and let the detectives handle it."

"That's easy for them to say!" Redcliff almost shouted. "It's not their daughter who's in danger!"

"Take it easy, Brad! We still have a little over two days to find her."

"Don't tell me what to do, John!"

Josh looked anxiously at his father, who took a slow, deep breath. "Let's go inside and get a soft drink," he suggested, heading toward the service station. "When we finish, it'll be time to try Chow again."

As Josh and Tank started to follow, Melanie's father said contritely, "I'm sorry, John. I'm not thirsty, but if it's okay, I'll join you. I don't want to be alone."

When Josh, his father, and Tank had bought their beverages and stood by the phone booth drinking them, Josh saw that his father was deep in thought.

Josh asked, "What're you thinking, Dad?"

He lowered his voice so only Josh could hear. "One of the reasons Mr. Chow hadn't been able to get the information is because of what I'd told you in confidence earlier."

"You mean about the stolen nuclear bomb?" When his father nodded, Josh added, "I thought that was a big secret."

"It is, but I felt that it might possibly have a tie-in with Melanie's disappearance, so in the hotel room, while Brad talked to the other detective, Pim, I took Mr. Chow to one side and told him what I knew.

"He just now told me that local and federal authorities have to focus on this bomb situation. He wouldn't confirm anything about the nuclear device, but he did admit they're working on a bomb scare. However, they're not going to neglect Melanie's disappearance."

"I don't see why the police object to our us trying to find Melanie."

"The police naturally believe that they know better how to do certain things. No matter what stories you see on television about amateur sleuths beating the cops in solving a case, it doesn't happen that way in real life. Usually, amateurs mess things up."

"Are you going to tell Mr. Redcliff?"

"That's what I'm debating. He's getting so upset and short-tempered that I may have to tell him so he'll understand better." Mr. Ladd looked at his wristwatch. "Well, it's time to call Detective Chow back."

Josh was apprehensive as he rejoined Tank and Redcliff while Josh's dad made his call. The boys and Melanie's distraught father stood silently around until Mr. Ladd hung up the phone.

He reported, "Mr. Chow is very busy on another case, but he asked a fellow detective to check on the information we wanted. The license plate on the black sedan showed it was a rental. The driver gave his name as Peka Kunu,* and his home address at Waimea."

"Waimea?" Redcliff cried. "Isn't that where your friend Palmer lives on the Big Island?"

Mr. Ladd nodded and continued. "The young detective also found that the black sedan had been returned to the rental agency at the Honolulu airport. I assume that means at least the driver is returning to his home."

"Then let's go to the Big Island!" Redcliff exclaimed, heading for Mr. Ladd's car. "John, we'll talk to this Peka Kunu and also to your friend Palmer."

"Not so fast, Brad!" Mr. Ladd cautioned. "Chow said that authorities on the Big Island will go to Kunu's address to contact him. We're to stay away."

"I can't do that!" Redcliff yelled, slapping his hands together in anger. "I have to do everything possible to find Melanie!"

"We don't want the police upset with us," Mr. Ladd said evenly. "We can talk to my friend Olin Palmer, but that's all."

"Nothing's going to stop me from doing what I can to find my daughter!" Redcliff said heatedly. "If you don't want to get involved, just give me your friend's address and drop me off at the airport."

Mr. Ladd hesitated. Josh caught his eye and realized he was making a tough decision.

"Brad," Josh's father said, shifting his gaze to the other man, "I understand your frustration. But there's something you don't know, so let's all get in the car and I'll tell you. I don't want anyone to overhear."

Settled inside the rented vehicle, Mr. Ladd didn't reach for the ignition. Instead, he turned to where he could look at all three other occupants.

"Brad," he began, "and you too, Tank, I want your solemn promise that you won't tell anyone else what I'm going to share with you."

When the promises were made, Mr. Ladd explained. "The authorities have another terrible case on their hands right now. The Pono Paha has threatened to detonate a bomb in Hawaii— and it may be a nuclear one."

Tank exclaimed in disbelief, "Where could they get one of those bombs?"

Josh was tempted to blurt out the source his father had mentioned earlier, but decided he would be breaking his promise if he indicated he already knew something about that. Instead, he joined the others in looking expectantly at Mr. Ladd.

"That's not important right now," he said with a shrug. "While authorities privately consider the Pono Paha claims so outrageous as to be unbelievable, there is a certain caution. It's possible that some nuclear weapons have been smuggled out of the former Soviet Union to unknown buyers.

"So the point is that authorities believe Mano of the Pono Paha has such a weapon or at least conventional bombs. They're not taking any chances that he's bluffing. Anyway, Mano has sent a warning to civil and military authorities in the island, setting a time limit for decolonization, as he calls it."

"You're kidding!" Redcliff exclaimed. "When?"

"Mano didn't say exactly, but sometime after Saturday noon."

"After it's too late for Melanie," her father said hoarsely.

"Don't give up on us finding her, Brad," Josh's father urged. He hesitated, then continued. "The Pono Paha group demands that prompt state measures be taken to stop development of land that dissidents consider sacred. That includes Japanese-owned golf courses and businesses owned by us haoles. In fact, all foreigners are to be forced off the islands so original islanders may return to self-government."

"And if this edict isn't obeyed?" Redcliff prompted.

"Mano of Pono Paha warns that unless his demands are carried out immediately, he'll ruin the state's nine billion dollar tourist industry by detonating one or more small portable nuclear bombs at the islands' airports. Even the threat will drastically reduce the number of visitors. They wouldn't dare come here under those circumstances."

"And your business would be ruined," Josh said.

"So would my dad's," Tank added quickly. His father managed the Honolulu branch of one of the nation's largest department stores. "But maybe it's a bluff."

"It might be," Redcliff admitted, "But after what happened to Melanie and me, I guess it is possible."

"I'm sure the authorities are taking it very seriously, Brad," Mr. Ladd said. "Naturally, the public at large can't be told. There could be a panic. The authorities want to handle this thing quietly."

Redcliff said, "I understand their problem, and that they'll have to put every available officer on that bomb threat. But they'd better understand that no matter what they say, I'm going to find my daughter!"

Josh exclaimed without thinking, "I'll help you!" He turned to his father, asking, "Won't we, Dad?"

"Of course, but, Brad, promise me that you'll not interfere with the police investigation."

"I'm not promising anything, John, except to find Melanie, even if I have to do it alone! Is that clear?"

"Yes, perfectly." Mr. Ladd answered quietly. "But you'll

only get in trouble with the police if they think you're interfering. The boys and I want to help you, but we can't if you don't obey the detectives' orders."

Josh felt his keen disappointment at the possibility of not being able to go on searching for Melanie. He fingered the scholarship pin on his shirt, thinking, *I shouldn't care after what she did to me, but I do.*

Redcliff took a deep breath. "I'm sorry, John," he said contritely. "I'm just so upset I'm saying foolish things. Please forgive me, and come with me."

Josh glanced anxiously at his father, who slowly nodded. "On the conditions I've outlined, Brad?"

When Redcliff agreed, hurried phone calls were made. It was dark when necessary arrangements were completed and Josh, his father, Tank, and Redcliff rushed through the boarding gates at Honolulu. Their inter-island plane had stopped over from Kauai to discharge and take on passengers bound for Kailua-Kona.*

The two fathers took seats on the left side of the aisle. Across the aisle Tank slid into the window seat on the right. Josh started to sit beside him, then his eyes widened at a passenger sitting three rows back

"Tank!" Josh whispered hoarsely, dropping heavily into his seat. "Opu Nui is right behind us!"

Chapter Eight

SHADOWS IN THE NIGHT

As Tank started to raise up in his seat, Josh warned in a hoarse whisper, "Don't look now!"

"Opu Nui won't recognize you or me," Tank protested in a low voice.

"Probably not, but the way he was staring at Melanie's father, I'm sure Opu recognized him. When my dad sat down with Mr. Redcliff, and we sat across . . ."

"Yeah!" Tank interrupted, still in a low tone. "Opu will figure out that we're together. Now what'll we do?"

Josh's mind raced as the flight attendants began their demonstration of the aircraft's safety features which Josh had seen many times on previous flights. He kept his voice low to share his thoughts with Tank.

"Opu can't do anything while we're on the plane, and I don't want to be too obvious by leaning across the aisle and telling Dad."

"Opu sure gets around," Tank answered. "Since we saw him today here on Oahu, he's been to Kauai, and now he's going to the Big Island. Do you suppose he's meeting with Holo?"

"It's possible. Incidentally, his real name is Peka Kunu. But I wonder why Opu went to Kauai? And what's he going to do now that he sees us together?"

Tank said he didn't know, so when the plane landed, Josh quickly stood in the aisle behind his father and alerted him to the situation.

Mr. Ladd didn't look around, but allowed Josh, Tank, and Melanie's father to precede him toward the front of the aircraft and into the terminal. Knowing that Opu was behind, watching, made the short hairs on the back of Josh's neck crawl. *I wonder what he will do now?*

Out of the corner of his eye, Josh saw that Opu didn't go toward the baggage claim area. Instead, carrying only a small brief case, he hurried to his left, passed one car-rental office and entered the next.

Mr. Ladd said crisply, "Good! He's not going to the same agency as we are. You three keep an eye on him while I get our car. Then let's hope we can follow him and see where he goes."

Without waiting for anyone to answer, Mr. Ladd took long-legged strides toward the first car-rental office. Josh joined Tank and Melanie's father in watching the next agency where Opu had gone.

Tank said, "Your dad wants to follow Opu Nui, but what if he's planning to follow us?"

"That'll be interesting," Josh replied.

He felt some concern when his father came running back to say that the rented car wouldn't be brought to him, as he expected. Instead, he'd have to take a shuttle bus to where the car was parked several blocks away.

He concluded, "So keep an eye out for that man when he comes out again. See which way he goes, and I'll be back as soon as possible."

As the minutes stretched on, Josh's anxiety began to build. His father didn't return, and Opu did not leave the car-rental office.

Finally Redcliff said, "I don't understand that. Would one of you boys run over and peek inside the office where Opu is? See what's taking him so long. I'd go, but he might see me, so I'll wait here for John."

Josh volunteered. He dashed across the black lava area that had been paved and cautiously walked by the car-rental's small office. Josh was in the darkness, but it was light in the office. He stopped, frowning.

That's strange! He's not there!

Josh hurried back to report to Tank and Redcliff as Josh's father pulled up in a blue four-door sedan. Josh briefly reported his finding. He concluded, "Opu Nui must have slipped out the back door at the rental office and got into his rental car. But did he drive away, or is he hanging back somewhere, waiting to follow us?"

After some discussion, the two men and two boys decided there was no choice but to proceed with their original plan. They headed south, passed through the historic community of Kailua-Kona and followed Highway 11 to a condominium a short way out of town.

The widowed owner of one unit was a member of the same California church as the Ladds. She had arranged for the family to use her condo when she was on the Mainland, as now.

Josh kept twisting his head to see if any car seemed to be following. It was hard to tell when all he could see were headlights in the night. After passing several other condos along the shore, Mr. Ladd slowed by the hedge of bougainvillea* that marked the entrance to the condo, Josh sighed. "Now what, Dad?"

"I'll pull into the underground parking lot and run upstairs to get the key. You three could get out of the car and stand over in the shadows to see if Opu follows us. If he does, don't let him see you."

Josh was still excited when his father returned minutes later with the key. "Any sign of Opu?" Mr. Ladd asked, joining them behind a large concrete block pillar.

"Nobody's gone in or out," Josh reported.

"So maybe he didn't follow us," Melanie's father commented. "That means we've lost one possible lead to finding my daughter."

"Or maybe Opu saw us turn in here," Tank observed, looking around nervously, "and he pulled into one of the other condos along here. He could be watching us now."

Mr. Ladd and Redcliff agreed that was possible, but there was no way of knowing. With everyone agreeing to be careful, they took the elevator to the third floor.

The condo was built around a garden with a running

stream filled with brightly colored koi* separating the two parallel wings. Brilliant red ginger blossoms and other colorful flowers grew along the well-tended banks. The unit had a kitchen, two bedrooms, and a combination living and dining room that opened onto a small lanai.

Since everyone was too excited to sleep, they slid the wide screen door back and stepped out onto the 12-foot by 12-foot square lanai. They didn't turn on the outside lights in order to better see the ocean a hundred yards away. There floodlights illuminated the tumbled black lava and waves that crashed ashore, breaking into white spray.

For awhile, no one spoke. The night was filled with the crash of surf and the sound of cars passing along the highway.

Finally, Melanie's father jumped up. "I can't stand this!" he cried hoarsely. "I'm sitting here in this peaceful setting like a tourist when time is running out on my daughter's life!"

"Easy, Brad, easy!" Mr. Ladd said soothingly. He stood up and put his hand on the other man's shoulder. "There's nothing we can do until morning!"

"I know that!" Redcliff said in a sad voice. "But it's driving me crazy anyway."

Josh felt great sympathy for Melanie's father, but didn't know how to console him.

Mr. Ladd asked, "Brad, would you like me to pray with you?"

Redcliff took a slow, shuddering breath. "I can't remember the last time I prayed. But if that's the only thing we can do. . . ." He let his sentence trail off, then added,

"Could we go inside? Just you and me, John?"

After the men had gone into the living room, Josh and Tank fell into a thoughtful silence.

Both kept an anxious eye on the open land between the lanai and the next condo separated by a high bamboo hedge. Each property was lighted with small electric bulbs hidden along the walkways leading to the ocean. A few visitors strolled down and then back to enter their individual condo units.

Finally Tank said softly, "I wonder if Opu Nui is out there, waiting for us to go to sleep?"

"Even if he is," Josh replied, "there's no reason to worry about it. He and his partner saw Dad's car registration, so they knew where we live. If they wanted to do something to us, they could have done it there when we were asleep. They may just be trying to scare us off, or they may only want to keep an eye on us."

"Then how come Mano and his Pono Paha people grabbed Melanie instead of us?"

"I suppose because they want to punish her father for investigating their organization. Or maybe it has something to do with their beliefs. The Pono Paha movement is pretty far out, you know."

Tank nodded. "What'd you think Opu's doing now?"

"My guess is that he's probably wondering what we're doing here. Maybe he plans to follow us tomorrow."

"Or maybe sneak up on us while we sleep tonight," Tank muttered. "I don't like it."

Neither did Josh, but he fell silent, letting his eyes roam

the shadows on the grounds below. Behind him, he could hear his father's voice through the screen door.

Suddenly, Josh tensed. "Look, Tank!" Josh leaned forward in his chair, pointing over the lanai railing. "There by the bamboo! Someone's moving!"

He and Tank watched in tense silence as a man slipped out of the bamboo. He moved cautiously toward the condo, taking advantage of the shadows cast by the decorative lights placed along the walkway.

"It's him!" Tank exclaimed in a hoarse whisper. "Opu Nui! I see his big belly! He must have followed us from the airport after all. He's coming this way."

When the furtive figure moved out of sight below the condo, Josh exclaimed, "Let's go see what he's up to."

Tank groaned. "No! Let's stay here!"

Josh stood up. "You can if you want, but I'm going."

With a weary sigh, Tank muttered, "Why can't I have a best friend who's a coward?"

Josh didn't reply, but slipped inside the screen door, followed by Tank. Josh started to tell his dad what he planned to do, but his eyes were closed and his lips moved in prayer. Redcliff's head was bowed.

Josh eased out the front door, closing it gently behind him. "We'll only be a minute," he told Tank and looked over the side of the walkway and to the left. Opu was entering the open lobby at the front of the building.

Breathlessly, the boys dashed down the stairs and along the garden to where they could see the front desk. Only the pretty brown-skinned clerk in her red and yellow muumuu was there.

Tank whispered, "Where'd he go?"

"Let's go ask her." After making sure that Opu Nui wasn't around, Josh and Tank hurried up to desk.

"Did a man with a big potbelly come here a minute ago?" Josh asked, leaning across the desk.

"Oh, yes. He said he was looking for a friend. Then he described someone I'd never heard of."

Tank whispered, "Melanie's father."

"When I said I didn't recognize the description," the clerk continued, "he said his friend was with another man, and he described your father, Josh. I offered to let him use the house phone to call, but he just left."

Josh and Tank exchanged glances, then both turned back to the clerk. "Where did he go?" Josh asked.

"Down the stairs and to the left, toward the garage. Why? Is anything wrong?"

"I hope not," Josh answered. "But would you mind phoning my dad? Tank and I will try to catch up . . . no, wait!" He turned to Tank. "I don't want to disturb them right now, yet Dad should know what's going on. Will you run up and tell him?"

"What about you?"

"I'll follow Opu."

"I don't like it!" Tank protested.

Josh gave him a gentle shove. "I'll be careful. Now, hurry!"

Alone in the underground garage with its echoing concrete walls and dim overhead fluorescent lights, Josh silently ran on bare feet. He soon caught sight of Opu Nui moving toward the far end of the garage nearest the ocean. *Where's he going?* Josh wondered.

Opu seemed unaware that he was being followed. He left the garage through a pedestrian exit and took the dimly lit footpath toward the ocean. Carefully, Josh followed, slipping stealthily along on bare feet toward where he could hear the waves pounding the black shore.

Pausing occasionally to listen, and satisfied that he was still hearing Opu's footsteps ahead of him, Josh continued seaward. He could dimly make out the lights of cottages perched on the great black masses of tumbled lava just beyond where the breakers crashed ashore.

With rapidly beating heart and wishing Tank were along, Josh followed until the crash of the waves made it impossible to hear Opu's footfalls. *Guess I should turn back,* Josh told himself, *but maybe Opu will do something that leads us to Melanie.*

Josh moved on until he saw a small cottage with an outside light burning weakly above the front entrance.

Josh cautiously eased forward, trying to see Opu by the light reflected back toward the pathway.

Josh stopped, swallowed hard, and looked around with growing anxiety. *Where did he go?*

Josh heard a furtive footstep behind him and started to whirl around.

It was too late.

A big hand closed over his mouth and a powerful arm encircled his body, crushing the breath out of him.

Chapter Nine

FOLLOWING A CLUE

Josh instinctively twisted away from the crushing arm about his body. At the same time, he twisted his head sideways and freed his mouth from Opu's smothering hand.

Instantly, Josh yelled wildly while shoving mightily against his attacker's chest. Opu Nui took a step backward and tripped over one of the small lights illuminating the path. He fell hard, crashing heavily into some variegated ivy growing beside the path.

Josh turned and ran frantically back along the pathway the way he'd come. He heard Opu swear, regain his feet, and pound noisily after him.

An older woman, apparently investigating Josh's yell, turned on an outside light and stepped out on the lanai of her second-floor condo. Without slowing, Josh yelled up at her, "Call the police! He's after me!"

Josh dashed on, deciding to run straight along the condo toward the street rather than take a chance on Opu catching him alone in the underground garage. Headlights of passing cars showed above the bougainvillea hedge, marking the end of the condo grounds.

Josh could hear Opu's labored breathing, mixed with swearing and threats. *He's gaining on me!* Josh's frenzied thoughts urged him to turn the corner of the condo when he got there and run up to the desk.

No, he told himself, *the lady clerk can't help me, and I'll never get to our unit before Opu catches me!*

He dashed past the front end of the condo and across the driveway leading away from the underground garage. He raced through the well-lit entrance between the bougainvillea hedges onto the highway. A break in the moderate traffic approaching from both directions allowed Josh to sprint across the road. He started running toward the first set of headlights, praying he wouldn't get hit.

This oncoming car's headlights momentarily blinded him. Josh threw up his hands to protect his eyes just as brakes squealed. The car locked up and skidded sideways.

Josh risked a quick glance back. His pursuer had almost been hit by the car. As the driver stopped sideways across the center of the road, he angrily shouted at Opu, who turned and ran back into the condo grounds. Josh slowed his pace, breathing hard, while the irate driver straightened out his vehicle and drove on, yelling loudly in the night. Opu disappeared around the side of the condo.

He's probably going to cut back through the bamboo to wherever he parked his car, Josh decided. He looked up at the overcast sky. "Thanks, Lord," he whispered.

Some time later, Josh was safely back in the condo unit.

The police came, vainly searched for Opu Nui, took Josh's statement, and left.

"Son," Josh's father said sternly, "you should never have followed that man alone. There's no telling what might have happened."

"I'm sorry, Dad. I didn't think." Josh gingerly touched his mouth where Opu's hand had brutally closed over it. His lips were slightly puffy.

Tank asked, "Do you think he'll come back tonight?"

The two fathers looked at each other, then shook their heads.

"No," Redcliff answered. "I don't think Opu will risk that. I think he's long gone."

"I hope you're right, Brad," Josh's dad said. "But since they didn't succeed in grabbing Josh to make him tell where we're going, the only way they can find out now is to follow us in the morning."

"You're right, John," Redcliff agreed. "But to do that, Opu would have to hide someplace where he could watch this condo when we left. Because there's no other exit except the one out front, he could be planning to wait in his car for us to leave."

To prevent that possibility, it was decided that everyone would get up early and head for Olin Palmer's place by daybreak.

Before dawn, with Melanie's father in the front passenger seat, Mr. Ladd steered the rented sedan out of the condo grounds and headed for Kailua-Kona. Josh was wide awake in the back seat, but Tank was still sleepy.

Josh joined his father and Redcliff in watching carefully to see if Opu was following them. He didn't seem to be, but in town Josh's father made several turns onto side streets. Satisfied that nobody was tailing them, he circled around to pick up Highway 190 and headed inland without stopping for breakfast.

They soon passed miles of small clumps of grass that reminded Josh of drawings he had seen of gnomes. When he asked his father about the grass, he replied that these were plants imported from Africa. He concluded, "So much of what we have in Hawaii isn't indigenous."

"What's that?" Josh asked.

"Oh, something that originates in a particular country, or native to a particular region."

"Sort of like us," Tank said with a yawn. "The kind that Mano and his Pono Paha people want to get rid of."

Josh glanced at Melanie's father. His eyes seemed puffy. Josh guessed he'd been awake much of the night.

"Only a day-and-a-half left," Redcliff said soberly.

"We've still got time," Josh answered with as much confidence as possible. "We'll find her."

Melanie's father didn't answer, but leaned against the back of the front seat and closed his eyes. He didn't open them until Josh's father spoke again.

"Boys," he said, "we're passing the famous Parker Ranch. I understand that it's the largest privately owned cattle ranch in the world, with more than a quarter-million acres.

Look around and see if you can spot any Hawaiian cowboys. They're called paniolos."*

Josh swept his eyes from the massive bulk of Mauna Kea* to the right back to the ocean, which was visible to the left. "I only see some horses but no cattle," he observed as the car continued on.

In Waimea, Mr. Ladd parked in front of a small cafe. He said, "You boys order a quick breakfast for yourselves, but only coffee for me. I'm going to ask directions to Olin Palmer's place. Brad, you'd better eat something."

"I'll also just have coffee," he replied as Josh's father walked to the heavyset cashier. Redcliff lowered his voice and looked at the boys. "I know you two must be starved, but I'd appreciate it if you ate quickly so we can find this friend of your fathers."

He sat down at a table where Josh and Tank ordered hot malasadas,* which were ready to serve. The waitress poured Mr. Ladd's coffee just as he returned and sat down with a frown.

"What's the matter, Dad?" Josh asked.

"Olin's moved."

Redcliff groaned. "You mean that we've come all this way for nothing?"

"Maybe not, Brad," Mr. Ladd said. "He's now living near Waipio Valley Overlook."

"Is that far from here?" Melanie's dad asked.

"Not far, Brad." He picked up his coffee. "The man at the counter drew a map on this napkin. I think we can find Olin after we finish breakfast."

Back in the car Mr. Ladd turned onto Highway 19 leading toward Honokaa,* then swung left onto Highway 240 which ran inland just above the shoreline. Following the crude map, they eventually found a small dirt road leading toward the ocean. Mr. Ladd parked in front of a rusted metal cable stretched across the unpaved, rutted driveway.

"I guess we walk from here," Mr. Ladd said, sliding out of the car.

Josh also got out, looking down the narrow drive about a hundred yards toward the ocean. A small frame house with rusted corrugated roof had been built under an immense tree less than 50 feet from the ocean.

"Somebody's coming out of the house," Josh announced as Tank and Redcliff closed the car doors. "A lady."

"Probably Olin's wife," Mr. Ladd guessed. "She's certainly a striking-looking woman."

Josh saw that she was about six feet tall with a stately bearing. "Hele mai. Hele mai,"* she called.

"What's that mean?" Josh asked.

"It probably means, 'Come on' or 'come in.' Remember, I told you Olin had married an island girl."

When they approached the woman, Josh saw that her body was well proportioned to her height. She had pale brown skin, loose black hair streaked with gray, and soft, warm, dark eyes. She smiled in welcome and said, "You must be looking for my husband."

"Are you Mrs. Palmer?" Josh's father asked. When she

nodded, he added, "Olin and I knew each other in California a long time ago. It's very important that we talk to him right away."

"Oh, I'm sorry," she replied, "but he just took the four-wheeler* and headed for Waipio Valley for a few days to camp and hike with our youngest son, Lopaka."*

Josh heard Melanie's father say something sharply under his breath. Josh glanced at him. His face had turned pale and his shoulders sagged heavily.

Mr. Ladd said, "Mrs. Palmer, is there any way we can find him?"

She shook her shoulder-length hair, making it shimmer down her back. "Not with that sedan you're driving," she answered as Josh's father reached out to grip Redcliff's arm. "Unless maybe," she added, "you can catch him before he enters the valley. He and Lopaka had to stop at a store . . ."

"Which store?" Redcliff broke in, suddenly straightening up in obvious hope.

After Mrs. Palmer had given directions, Redcliff started trotting toward the car. Josh started to follow as his father lingered a moment. "Mrs. Palmer, in case we miss Olin, please tell him that John Ladd was here. He'll remember me. I'm sorry we haven't time to explain."

On the fast drive toward the small store Mrs. Palmer had described, Josh's father said grimly, "If Olin enters the valley before we find him, we can't follow. I remember that only four-wheel-drive vehicles can go there, and rental cars can't be taken onto unpaved roads. So let's hope we're not too late."

When his father stopped at the small store, Josh looked around quickly. "No four-wheel-drives here."

His father replied, "I'll run inside and make sure."

He was back in less than a minute. "Olin left about five minutes ago," he announced, starting the motor.

Redcliff asked anxiously, "Can we catch him before he enters the valley?"

"We're going to try. Fortunately, I know the way."

The road was narrow, and Josh's father drove fast enough that the tires squealed going around curves.

Josh turned to Melanie's father. He leaned his head wearily against the back of the front seat. Josh couldn't see his face, but he could imagine his disappointment.

"Don't give up hope, Mr. Redcliff," Josh urged.

Melanie's father didn't answer, so Josh fell silent with the others until they reached the parking lot marking the end of the paved but deserted road. Mr. Ladd stopped in the roadway before the entrance to Waipio Valley. Signs posted there warned that no passenger cars could pass this point.

To the left, Josh heard a rooster crowing on a small farm. On the right, there was a small parking lot with only one luxury sedan. An older man and a woman stood at the railing, looking through binoculars at the distant waterfall on the ocean-facing cliffs.

"Too late," Melanie's father whispered in one of the saddest tones Josh had ever heard. "We're too late."

"Maybe not," Mr. Ladd said, sliding out of the car. "I'll ask that couple if they've seen anything."

Josh, Tank, and Redcliff remained silently in the car until Mr. Ladd hurried back and stuck his head through the open front passenger window.

"Those people said they weren't really paying any attention, but some kind of a vehicle entered a few minutes ago."

Josh couldn't look at Melanie's father, knowing how badly his hopes had been crushed. Instead, Josh lifted his eyes to his father. "What do we do now?"

He sighed and started to answer, then swung around to look back down the road they'd just driven. "Here comes a four-wheel vehicle."

Josh exclaimed, "There's a man and a boy inside."

Tank started walking rapidly with Josh as he and Redcliff exited the car and faced the oncoming vehicle. It slowed and stopped.

Mr. Ladd ran around to the open driver's side window. "Olin!" he cried. "Thank God, we've found you!"

Olin Palmer was a very tall man with a deep tan, blue eyes, and sandy-colored beard. His son was about 11. He had a slender build, light brown skin, black hair, and brown eyes. After the men had shaken hands, everyone was introduced, including Lopaka, Palmer's son.

The boys said hi to each other, then Mr. Palmer turned to Josh's dad. "Now, John," he asked, "what brings you here with such an anxious face?"

Mr. Ladd briefly explained, concluding, "So, Olin, do you know of a place called Forbidden Falls?"

"No," Palmer replied thoughtfully, "but I've heard about a place called Kapu Falls.* Kapu means 'forbidden' in English."

Melanie's father said eagerly, "That has to be the same place. That's probably where they're holding my daughter. So where is it?"

"I don't know exactly, but I'm sure that it's not on this island," Palmer replied.

"Then where is it?" Redcliff demanded.

"Well," Palmer explained, "my father-in-law mentioned it to me a long time ago . . ."

"Your father-in-law?" Tank interrupted. "Is he really a kahuna?"

"He's a real Hawaiian," Palmer said, "but my wife doesn't like me to refer to him as a kahuna. However, he is one of the kapunas,* or wise Hawaiian elders."

"Never mind that!" Redcliff said bluntly. "Where is this Kapu Falls?"

"On Kauai."

Josh saw Melanie's father reel as though he'd been struck a physical blow. "I've got to find it!"

"Hold on!" Palmer protested. "I understand your concern, Mr. Redcliff, but you can't go there."

"Why not? If Melanie's there, I'm going to get her!"

"There are a couple of reasons. First, it's sacred to the old Hawaiians, so no haole, including me, has ever been allowed to go there. Second, its exact location is a closely guarded secret."

Josh's hopes for rescuing Melanie before Mano's deadline vanished.

Chapter Ten

A WILD RACE

What?" Melanie's father shouted in disbelief. "Are you serious? Nobody knows where to find Kapu Falls?"

"That's right," Palmer replied. "At least, no haole does, and many Hawaiians probably don't either."

Redcliff plunged on. "And no white person is allowed there because the falls are sacred to the old Hawaiians?"

Palmer nodded. "I'm afraid so."

"Well, *I'm* going to find that place!" Redcliff shouted angrily. "I'm going to rescue my daughter before Saturday noon. Somehow, I'm going to do it!"

Josh's father and Mr. Palmer tried to calm the distraught man, but he shook them off. He paced up and down in front of the entrance to Waipio Valley.

Josh noticed the older couple in the parking lot abruptly stop looking at the distant waterfalls. They hurriedly returned to their car and drove away.

Josh's gaze returned to Melanie's father as he stopped shouting. He seemed about to collapse. Mr. Ladd and Palmer assisted Redcliff toward the rental sedan.

Josh shifted his eyes to Tank and Lopaka, motioning for them to follow him to the parking lot.

They stopped at the railing overlooking the valley with the high cliffs and the waterfall above the surf.

Lopaka pointed. "See that valley? Years ago, a big tidal wave came in from the sea." His finger moved to the right where whitecaps were breaking over a sandy beach. "The tsunami* rushed inland and carried away all the people who lived there."

Josh nodded, not particularly interested because of his concern about Melanie. *There's got to be a way to find and rescue her before it's too late,* he told himself, letting his eyes drift up from the valley below. He could make out faint, narrow trails on the sides of the steep hills rising on the far side of the valley.

Josh remembered the earlier discussion about Waipio Valley. He forced his mind away from Melanie and commented, "I heard that the natives believed that the entrance to the Hawaiian underworld was back there."

Lopaka nodded gravely. "My grandpa, the kahuna, used to tell me stories about that."

"Yeah?" Tank prompted.

"Yeah. He said that on the darkest night when there was no moon, the entrance to the underworld would open and the spirits would come out. The kahunas were supposed to be able to see the spirits."

Josh frowned. He didn't believe in spirits, but he had lived in Hawaii long enough not to show his feelings to those who held different beliefs.

Lopaka added in a somber tone, "That was the night all the ordinary people would sit in their huts, shaking from fear."

Josh glanced toward the three men. They had gotten inside Mr. Ladd's rental car with Melanie's father between them. He had his head in his hands.

Tank asked Lopaka, "Is it true that King Kamehameha grew up not far from here?"

"Uh-huh. He went to school at Waipio Valley when he was a boy. Later, he went away to train for war. When he was grown, he conquered all the different chiefs in all the Hawaiian islands and united them under him."

Josh nodded absently, knowing the story. "He died just about when the first haole missionaries came from Boston, and his favorite wife helped them Christianize the islands."

Tank declared, "Well, there aren't as many Christians here today as there are believers in other religions! Yet that's not surprising, considering how many people came here from foreign countries."

Josh's mind snapped back to Melanie. "Lopaka, do you think your grandfather would know where Kapu Falls are?"

"Even if he did," the boy replied somberly, "he wouldn't tell."

"Not even to save a girl's life?"

Lopaka shrugged. "I guess you could ask him, only he's gone to the Mainland. I don't know just where."

The boys continued their conversation until Mr. Palmer got out of the car and motioned to them. On coming close, Josh could see that Melanie's father had a puffy face and red eyes.

Been crying, Josh thought. *Well, I almost feel like that myself. Poor Melanie!*

"Before we go," Mr. Ladd said to his old friend, "is there anything you can tell us about this Mano? I mean, what makes him the way he is?"

Olin Palmer shrugged. "He's a very mysterious character, so nobody knows who he really is or what makes him tick. But from what I've heard other kanaka maoli say, including some kapunas, for years, Mano and his family were very badly treated by haoles."

Redcliff spoke up. "I'd like to hear about that, but there isn't time. At least we now know that Forbidden Falls is on Kauai, so let's fly over there and try to find Melanie before it's too late."

Palmer nodded. "Of course." He turned to his son, "Run to the four wheeler and look under the front seat. I remember seeing an old newspaper there with some facts that might prove helpful to these people in trying to understand Mano and his whole kanaka maoli culture."

As Lopaka ran to obey, Mr. Ladd said, "Olin, I still remember the story you told me years ago about a leper who lived on Kauai."

Josh wanted to hear the story, but they needed to get moving, so Josh kept quiet. When Lopaka returned with the newspaper, Josh's father took it. Then everyone said goodbye. The Palmers continued on into Waipio Valley. Mr. Ladd headed the sedan back toward the airport at Kailua-Kona.

They rode awhile in silence. Josh felt sorry for Mr. Redcliff, but really ached inside for Melanie. He fingered the scholarship pin on his shirt, trying not to hurt so much.

After all, he told himself, *she cheated me out of this pin, and that's not right.* His silent reasoning didn't change how he felt. *I don't want her to die! If there was just some way we could find her! But there's so little time left.*

Finally Redcliff spoke. "John, your friend Palmer wasn't very encouraging about finding Forbidden Falls."

"Now, Brad, Olin was just trying to make you see how difficult a task it would be to find anybody on Kauai if that person were well hidden. Even if he were found, it'd be hard to reach him, because parts of Kauai are so remote and difficult to get to. That's how I remember the leper story Olin told me years ago."

Josh leaned forward a little more. Tank did the same. Both boys urged Mr. Ladd to tell the story.

"As I recall it," Josh's father began, "back in the days when leprosy* was hitting the native Hawaiians very hard, the authorities rounded up all those who had the disease and . . .

"Shipped them to Kalaupapa!"* Tank interrupted. "My dad and I have flown over that part of Molokai.* It sticks out like a sore thumb in the top middle of the island. Did you know they still have some lepers there?"

"Yes. It's called Hansen's Disease now," Mr. Ladd said. "But it's the same disease called leprosy in the Bible. Anyway, the story goes that in the old days, there was a man on Kauai with leprosy."

"So the authorities came to take the leper away, but he slipped off into the back of Kauai's Kalalau* Valley. There he held off all the authorities for months with just a single-shot rifle. They called him the Hermit of Kalalau, as I recall. Where that happened is not far from where the Na Pali* Coast State Park is today."

"I see the point you're making, John," Melanie's father said bittterly. "If someone wants to hide in the mountains of Kauai, it's about impossible to do anything about finding him. Palmer meant that the same is true about finding my daughter before Saturday noon."

"We'll do everything possible, Brad, but we must be aware of the obstacles we face," Mr. Ladd cautioned.

Redcliff asked, "Do you think we could find that driver who was arrested for following us too closely on Oahu? He lives around here, according to the police."

"Yes, Brad. But if we try to talk to him, the police would consider it interfering with their investigation."

"You're probably right," Redcliff agreed. "Let's get back to the airport as fast as we can. We sort of wasted the trip to this island, except we now know that Forbidden Falls is on Kauai. I'm not giving up on finding Melanie, so don't any of you quit, either."

The others assured him they wouldn't, although Josh had serious doubts. Still, he hoped and prayed as the car headed back down from the 2,000-foot elevation. They crossed miles of broken, open stretches of black lava where it seemed nothing could live, yet there were warning signs to look out for wild jackasses and goats.

At the sea level airport, Mr. Ladd dropped the others off at the airline terminal while he returned the rental car. Josh and Tank accompanied Melanie's father to buy tickets for a direct flight to Kauai, but there were none available.

When Mr. Ladd jogged back from returning the car, Redcliff hurriedly explained the situation. He concluded, "There's no choice but to go back to Honolulu and try to book a plane from there to Kauai."

As they waited for the Honolulu-bound inter-island jet, Josh looked around carefully, half expecting to see either Holo or Opu Nui. But when he saw no sign of them, Josh skimmed the newspaper that Palmer had given them and repeated what he had read to his attentive father, Tank, and Redcliff.

The general consensus among native Hawaiians was that they wanted more control over their lives and lands. Some wanted reparations, payment for what had been taken from their ancestors. Some wanted it known that the U.S. takeover a century ago had been illegal. Some wanted a nation within a nation, while others sought full independence. There were many reasons for each position.

Since the islands had first been discovered in 1778 by the British Explorer, Captain James Cook, native Hawaiians had gone down to the bottom of the socioeconomic ladder. Their life span was below the U. S. average.

Kanaka Maoli advocates wanted back nearly two million acres that had been ceded to the United States following the 1898 annexation. There were another 200,000 acres that had been set aside three-quarters of a century before for native Hawaiians to homestead. However, only a small fraction had ever been turned over to the native Hawaiians who had applied for them. They also wanted these lands, but many of those lands were occupied by the U.S. Navy and other government agencies.

Most of the various groups seeking independence or a nation within a nation did not advocate expelling all non-natives. Only a few dissident groups wanted that, with the Paha Pono the most radical advocate of that position.

Josh put the paper down and shook his head. "I can sure sympathize with them. They haven't been treated fairly, so if I were a native Hawaiian, I'd be angry."

"So would I," Redcliff said heatedly, "but this problem needs to be worked out peacefully, not as the Pono Paha group wants, threatening to disrupt the islands' economy with bombs, and especially not by taking Melanie's life."

The others agreed just as their flight was called. With a last look around to make sure that Holo and Opu Nui were not following them, Josh took his seat beside Tank.

Josh looked across the aisle at Melanie's father. His shoulders sagged with the terrible emotional burden he bore. His face was drawn and pale, and the pain of his thoughts transferred itself to Josh.

Josh sighed. "I wish there was some way we could get Holo or Opu Nui to tell us where Melanie is."

"Well, they'd never do that, even if we could talk to them. But you know what? Opu sure made a quick trip to Kauai and back yesterday. There wasn't much time from when the police stopped him and Holo outside of Honolulu until we saw Opu on the plane last night."

"That's true. Do you suppose he could have gone to Forbidden Falls in between those times?"

"He could by using a helicopter. Nothing's very far in one of those."

Josh sat up straight, thinking fast. "A helicopter!" His thoughts slipped back to chopper flights he had taken over the oldest island in the Hawaiian chain. Inland Kauai was filled with ancient valleys and immense peaks. Some were so high they scraped moisture from the clouds.

"The Garden Isle," Tank mused. "That's what they call it. Mighty pretty and green. And wet. The world's wettest spot is on that mountain right in the middle of the island."

"Mount Waialeale,"* Josh supplied the name. His mind jumped again. "If we could rent a helicopter, maybe we could fly over Kauai and find those Forbidden Falls."

"It'd be easier to find a needle in a haystack," Tank said.

Josh had to agree. He sighed and said, "It's too bad we couldn't have followed Opu Nui yesterday when he went to the falls."

"Yeah, but we'd have a fat chance of following him or anybody else to those falls before Saturday noon."

"Wait a minute!" Josh exclaimed, grabbing Tank's arm in sudden excitement. "There is someone we could follow!"

"Yeah? Who?"

"Kong!"

Chapter Eleven

DEADLINE DAY

King Kong?" Tank cried in disbelief.

"Yes! I just remembered he told me that he's going to be initiated into Pono Paha's Young Warriors Saturday morning. The place he mentioned was Kapu Falls. Maybe we can follow him straight to Melanie!"

Tank exclaimed, "Are you pupule,* Josh? All Kong ever does is beat up on us! He won't let us follow him."

"What if he doesn't know we're doing it?"

"How could you keep him from knowing?"

"I've got an idea. It's risky, but it's our only chance to save Melanie before it's too late."

Josh started to lean across the aisle to tell his father and Redcliff when the seat-belt sign came on. Josh had to wait until they'd landed.

As they left the plane and entered the terminal, Josh noticed more uniformed policemen than he'd ever seen at the airport before.

There were also a number of men and women in plain clothes who somehow didn't appear to Josh's sharp eyes to be passengers waiting for planes. They seemed to be moving casually, yet they lacked the purposeful walk of people really going or coming.

It also seemed to Josh that there were an unusual number of janitors, painters, and others in overalls or work clothes. They gave the appearance of going about their ordinary jobs, but Josh sensed they weren't actually working. Instead, they seemed to be watching or looking for something.

Nudging Tank, Josh whispered, "I think they're really officers working on the bomb scare."

"Well, I hope they find the bomb, if it's here. My hair's trying to stand on end just thinking of what would happen if that thing went off."

Josh was aware of a tenseness that made him want to get away from the airport as fast as possible. But first, he had to tell his father and Redcliff about his idea. As soon as they were out of the buildings, Josh motioned for them to stop where they couldn't easily be overheard. When he had finished, Melanie's dad frowned thoughtfully.

"Let's see if I have this right, Josh," he said. "Since Kong told you he was going to be initiated at Forbidden Falls day after tomorrow, that means we'd only have to follow him from the Kauai airport to the falls, wherever that is, instead of from his home."

"That's right," Josh agreed. "Opu or Holo or whoever takes Kong will have to have a helicopter waiting on Kauai to fly them to this secret place. It's a cinch they can't walk or drive, so we could follow them in another chopper."

Tank protested, "This is the rainy season, so trying to keep another 'copter in sight could be very hard. I remember my dad, who was a helicopter pilot in Vietnam, saying that there are often clouds and rain over Kauai's mountains. We might lose Kong in the sky somewhere."

Redcliff said thoughtfully, "Not if our chopper has radar, Tank." He shifted his attention to Josh. "This is already Thursday. I'll still do everything possible tomorrow, but if we haven't found Melanie by then, we'll have to try your idea. I'll hire a top-notch pilot while we're here at the airport."

Mr. Ladd said, "Let me call Tank's father. He flew choppers in Vietnam, and I'm sure that some of these pilots around here did the same. Maybe Sam can recommend one."

After talking with Sam Catlett at his office, Mr. Ladd announced, "He says to look up Jay Irwin, who owns his own charter company. Sam and he flew together in Vietnam, and this Irwin is a top pilot."

They hurried to where private planes and some helicopters were parked. Josh and Tank followed the two men into the small, cramped office with a sign reading, *Jay Irwin's Helicopter Charters.*

"I'm looking for Jay Irwin," Mr. Ladd said to the middle-aged man thumbing through a manual at the counter.

"You found him," the lanky, tousled-haired man behind the counter replied. "You must be John Ladd."

"Yes. How'd you know?"

"Sam Catlett called a minute ago. Said he'd just talked to you, but after he hung up, he decided it was important enough to call me and make sure I listened to your story." Irwin glanced at the boys. "Which of you boys is Sam's son?"

"I am," Tank replied. "This is Josh Ladd."

As the boys shook hands with the pilot, Mr. Ladd introduced Melanie's dad, who asked Irwin if he could fly them to Kauai.

The pilot nodded, saying that he had aircraft there for charter. When and where did they want to go?

Redcliff explained what he had in mind. He finished by asking, "Can you do that?"

"Can do," the pilot replied. He paused, then added, "I deeply sympathize with you, Mr. Redcliff."

"Call me Brad."

"Brad, I'm Jay."

Redcliff explained, "Jay, I'm going crazy knowing the time's going by so fast, so I don't want to waste a minute. I want you to fly us over to Kauai tomorrow and try to find this Forbidden Falls."

"Can't tomorrow," Irwin said, jerking his thumb over his shoulder at a radio. "Weather reports say we're going to have another heavy rainstorm like we had a few nights ago. Nothing except ducks are going to fly tomorrow until late in the day."

Josh saw the look of disappointment on Redcliff's face, but he struggled visibly to control himself. "Okay. Let's work out the details for Saturday," he said.

When this was done, the pilot again shook hands with Melanie's father saying, "If the authorities don't find your daughter before then, I'll see you all Saturday morning at Lihue*—that is, if the weather's clear."

Mr. Ladd phoned home to update his wife on the day's events. She reported that the garage had called to say the family station wagon was repaired. Even though it was late afternoon, they drove to the garage and picked it up. Redcliff drove the wagon back to the airport because Mr. Ladd's rental contract prohibited anyone but him from driving the car.

It was nearing dusk when Mr. Ladd took the wheel of his own vehicle and drove through downtown Honolulu to take Melanie's father to his hotel.

Their route took them past Queen Liliuokalani's statue between historic Iolani Palace and the state Capitol in downtown Honolulu. Colorful flower leis* decorated the monument to Hawaii's last ruling monarch.

"It's strange how things change," Josh's father commented. "When Hawaii was admitted as the fiftieth state in 1959, there were big celebrations. But 34 years later, on the one hundredth anniversary of Queen Liliuokalani being deposed, Hawaii's governor ordered the American flag removed from state buildings.

"He was quoted in a news story as saying something about it being important to remember the events that 'stole a nation.' I think those were his exact words. He urged the people to right that wrong. And Hawaii's longtime senator called the overthrow 'a dark page of our nation's history.'"

Melanie's father said bitterly, "I don't live in this state, and I'm not involved in their politics. So why did one radical group of dissidents have to kidnap my daughter and use her to make their point about people of Hawaiian ancestry?"

"Remember, Brad," Mr. Ladd said soothingly, "not everyone is a fanatic about this situation. Most people just want today's residents to be reminded of how the monarchy came to an end, and get justice now."

"Well, I don't care! I just want my daughter back."

Josh swallowed a lump that formed in his throat. He fingered the scholarship pin on his chest, wondering if he would ever see Melanie again.

She cheated me out of this, he reminded himself, *but I'd like to have a chance to give it back to her. What's a little old pin and my feelings compared to her life?*

That night, a mighty clap of thunder jerked Josh out of troubled sleep. He jumped out of bed and hurried to close the louvered windows of the room he shared with his little brother. Nathan didn't stir when sheet lightning lit up the whole sky, momentarily illuminating Diamond Head as bright as day.

That's when Josh saw the two men standing under a carport. The clap of thunder that followed the lightning didn't seem any louder to Josh than the sudden wild booming of his heart. *Is that Opu Nui and Holo?* he wondered, staring into the darkness and wishing for the sky to light up again. When it did, the men were gone.

At that moment, the sky seemed to burst, and rain fell in solid sheets. Each time lightning flashed, Josh's eyes desperately probed the carport and other areas below, but there was no sign of anyone. Josh began to wonder if he had just imagined seeing the two mysterious Pono Paha men.

Even if it was Opu Nui and Holo, Josh finally decided, *they may have just been trying to scare me by deliberately letting me see them. From that lightning flash, they must have seen me the same as I saw them. Once they did that, they probably left. I think it's safe to sleep again.*

With a prayer for protection for Melanie, himself, and the others, Josh lay down as the storm intensified. He drifted off to sleep again.

The thunder and lightning had passed but it was still raining lightly when Josh awoke. His first thought was that tomorrow noon was the deadline for finding Melanie, and today's weather would prevent any real efforts to locate her.

When Josh was dressed and ready for breakfast, the local television weatherman reported that 12 inches of rain had fallen on Oahu's windward side. Several head of cattle had been caught in a flash flood and washed down the hillsides toward the ocean. Waikiki's main street, famed Kalauka Avenue, had water up to the hubcaps of passing cars.

After Josh's father had asked the blessing, he announced plans to spend the day driving Brad Redcliff around, in spite of the bad weather. Their day would begin with a meeting of the detectives and FBI agents. They would probably have reports from officers on the Big Island who'd conducted investigations on Holo. There might be mug shots to look at to see if the real name of Opu Nui could be discovered.

"It'll probably take most of the day," Mr. Ladd concluded,

"so I imagine Brad's going to be really stressed out unless the authorities have some solid leads to Melanie's whereabouts."

"What about Tank and me?" Josh asked. "Should we go with you?"

"I don't think that's necessary. However, you and Tank should stay close to the apartments in case something comes up where you're needed."

After his father drove away in the rain, Josh went downstairs to Tank's apartment. They discussed whether Josh had really seen Opu Nui and Holo last night. Tank played some compact disks he'd received for Christmas, but mostly the boys stood and stared moodily out the window at the rain, hoping the detectives had good news about Melanie.

When the phone rang, Tank answered it and handed the instrument to Josh. "It's your mother."

Josh said hello and listened. "Your father just called. There's nothing new on Melanie's disappearance."

"I'm sorry," Josh said softly. "I really am."

"Your father says the forecasts call for clearing this afternoon, so he wants you to pack for the trip to Kauai tonight. You'd better tell Tank to do the same. Everyone has to be ready to board the helicopter when the first jet from Honolulu lands on Kauai tomorrow morning. Kong's probably going to be on that flight."

The sun had just set behind great cloud fragments of the passing storm when Josh and Tank followed Mr. Ladd and Melanie's father onto the inter-island jet bound for Lihue on Kauai. As they taxied on to the offshore runway, Josh looked out his window seat at the terminal and tower. *I wonder if the Pono Paha really will try to blow up the airport to prove their point?*

High in the air Josh nudged Tank sitting next to him. "Look! The sun's just setting again. I've never seen two sunsets in one day before."

When only great masses of clouds and a brilliant red glow marked the end of the second sunset, Josh's thoughts drifted to Melanie. "Noon tomorrow. Not much time left."

Josh and the others slept at a hotel near the Lihue airport and rose before dawn. Nobody spoke during breakfast, but Josh was sure they were all thinking the same thing. *By noon today it'll be over for Melanie unless our plan works and we can rescue her. I know Dad and Mr. Redcliff have talked with the pilot on how to do everything once we find Kapu Falls. But will we do that in time? What if something goes wrong?*

As Josh joined the others in boarding the shuttle to their helicopter, he fingered the scholarship pin on his shirt.

Tank's voice intruded into Josh's thoughts. "It's clouding up again."

"They're cumulus clouds," Mr. Ladd said soothingly. "Big and white and puffy, but I don't think there's any rain in them."

"You know how fast rain can come up, though," Tank answered.

"True," Josh's dad agreed. "Anyway, our pilot has radar, so we won't lose track of Kong's helicopter."

As dawn broke, the heliport was deserted except for Jay Irwin's big helicopter and a small red and white one a couple of hundred yards away.

Irwin said, "That's got to be the chopper waiting for the people you want to follow. Ray Phelps owns it. He was also with us in Vietnam. One of the best pilots in the business, and his aircraft is fast. So all of you had better get aboard so we can take off when Ray does."

Josh felt his heart begin to speed up as he joined the others in boarding. One seat remained empty, ready for Melanie if the rescue mission proved successful.

When seat belts were fastened and earphones adjusted for the noisy flight, everyone watched as the first inter-island jet from Honolulu landed.

"There they are!" Josh exclaimed upon spotting Kong with Holo and Opu as they disembarked and immediately headed for the smaller helicopter. As soon as they were aboard, the chopper quickly lifted off.

By comparison, Josh thought Jay Irwin's bigger, heavier helicopter was very slow. This seemed confirmed when Irwin was barely airborne. Kong's chopper was already a tiny speck in the distance, heading inland toward massive clouds.

Oh, no! Josh thought in sudden alarm. *We're losing them!*

Chapter Twelve

A SECRET UNCOVERED

In his earphones, Josh heard Mr. Redcliff's voice echoing his concern. "Jay, if we lose sight of that other chopper, we'll never find my daughter! And we have less than five hours left!"

The pilot spoke calmly into his microphone. "Relax, Brad! Remember, this baby has radar." He pointed to a pale green screen on the instrument panel. "See those three little blips? The two off to the left are sightseeing helicopters taking some visitors on an island tour. The sky'll soon be full of those, so Phelps will probably figure we're just another like them. The third blip straight ahead is Phelps' chopper."

Scanning the steep, green mountains ahead with their peaks lost in the clouds, Josh said, "I've heard about aircraft flying low to avoid radar. So what if your pilot friend dips down below some of those mountains?"

"Then," Irwin admitted, "we could have a problem unless we can maintain visual contact. Phelps's aircraft is small and fast. It holds only four, including the pilot. It does about 200 miles an hour, but doesn't have radar."

Irwin paused, then added, "Phelps's heading is directly toward Mount Wailaelae. That's 5,208 feet high and also the wettest spot on the face of the earth. So we may be hitting some rain in a minute."

With a touch of anxiety in his voice, Tank said, "Mr. Irwin, those mountain peaks we're flying over look like they're close enough to tear the bottom out of this helicopter."

"Relax," the pilot said, turning to give him a quick, reassuring smile. "I've been flying over these rain forests for years without incident. Try to enjoy the scenery. I'll watch the other chopper."

Josh had been feeling some concern himself, but he forced himself to look down at incredible valleys and soaring peaks appearing and disappearing as they flew into more and more clouds. Everything was green and beautiful. "No wonder they call Kauai the Garden Isle," he said.

Irwin pulled out a map and handed it and a pencil to Melanie's father sitting in the seat beside him. "You may want to look at this, Brad. When Phelps lands, I'll tell you where to mark the spot."

The chopper carrying Kong, Opu Nui, and Holo began veering right to avoid the great forested mountain where Josh could see rain now falling.

"According to this map," Redcliff commented, "we should soon be passing over several waterfalls."

"But none of those can be Forbidden Falls," Josh's father said. "Nobody knows where it is, so it must be well hidden."

Irwin asked, "How can a waterfall be hidden or unknown, considering how many helicopters cross and recross this island?"

Mr. Ladd replied, "That's pretty remote and desolate country down there. There's a lot of rain forest along with countless valleys between those mountain peaks."

Josh was aware that even though Irwin was now skirting the great mountain, the clouds became thicker and darker. Soon they made a solid cover, wiping out all the landscape in every direction, plus the other chopper.

Josh leaned forward to take another comforting look at the radar screen. "Hey!" he exclaimed into the microphone. "He's turned off to the left."

"No, that's a sightseeing chopper," Irwin said.

"Then where's the one with Kong?"

"It just went off the screen."

Redcliff demanded anxiously, "What's that mean?"

"It means Phelps has dropped down behind one of these mountains."

"Have we lost him?" Josh's father asked with a touch of concern in his voice.

"Not necessarily. He's probably starting his descent. I'll ease down out of these clouds and see if we can get a visual sighting on him again."

Redcliff exclaimed, "If we've lost . . ."

"Don't worry!" the pilot interrupted. "I know how important this mission is! Everyone keep a sharp lookout when we break out of this cloud cover."

Knowing all the high peaks with valleys between were everywhere, Josh tensed up, fearful of colliding with one of the green spires. *O Lord, don't let us hit one of those! Help us to find Kong's helicopter again, fast.*

A couple of anxious moments passed with only the heavy throbbing sound of the whirling overhead rotary blades. Then, through a hole in the clouds below and to the right, Josh caught a flash of reflected sunlight.

Josh pointed. "There they are!"

"Yes, I see," the pilot replied, banking his aircraft sharply. "Phelps has been following the contours of the earth, dodging mountainsides and lower peaks prior to landing."

Tank said hoarsely, "But there's no place to land! That's all jungle down there."

Josh's quick glance from the other aircraft to the earth below seemed to confirm his friend's observation. Confused, Josh looked back at the helicopter carrying Kong, Holo, and Opu Nui.

"He must see something," Josh commented, "because he's settling straight down. Yes, I see it—a little valley."

"He can't land in that tiny place," Tank exclaimed.

The other helicopter was settling into the top of a U-shaped opening so narrow the rotor blades seemed about to hit the sheer mountain sides.

"Relax, boys," Irwin urged. "I told you that Phelps is one of the best. He wouldn't be going down there if he wasn't confident that it could be done safely."

"Are we going to do that too?" Tank asked in a croak that

showed his fear.

"We may have to, but later," the pilot replied. "Right now, we want them to think we're just another sightseeing chopper." Irwin banked away and started climbing fast. "We'll gain some altitude to better see where they go after landing."

Although the abrupt turn caused gravity to force Josh back into his seat, he managed to keep an eye on the other helicopter. A moment later he announced, "He's landed safely."

Josh had some anxious moments as broken clouds swam lazily between his aircraft and the one on the ground. Then the three passengers left Phelps's helicopter. They bent nearly double to escape the rotary blast and started running across a small meadow. To Josh, they seemed like three tiny specks far below.

Almost instantly Phelps took off again, maneuvering up the narrow valley with the tips of his overhead rotor blades threatening to clip the mountain.

Irwin commented, "I should have realized they wouldn't take a haole like Phelps directly to their Forbidden Falls. The Pono Paha people wouldn't want him to know too much. But I don't see any waterfalls, so those three must plan to walk to wherever it is. Keep an eye on them and see where they go."

Josh's gaze flickered back and forth between the three people on the ground and the second helicopter. It rose straight up until it cleared the mountaintop and leveled off.

"Wow!" Tank breathed as Phelps's aircraft headed back toward Lihue. "I didn't think he'd make it."

"I told you he's good," Irwin replied. "But what he did, I can do."

"Wait!" Josh's father cried. "We can't take a chance on those people down there seeing us land."

The pilot assured him, "Once we know where those three on the ground are going, I'll land in one of those other nearby little valleys. You'll have to walk from there. If there are other people down there, they must have walked in from the outside. The ancient Hawaiians walked all over these islands. Traces of those old trails can still be found. Anyway, if those people down there now are the bad guys, as you all seem to think, they wouldn't dare risk having several helicopters flying in and out."

"Makes sense," Redcliff agreed. "But I'm concerned that this may not be the right place because there's no waterfall."

"Maybe there is, but we can't see it because we're at the wrong angle," Irwin replied. "I'll stay high and circle around so we won't arouse the suspicion of those on the ground. Watch both the people walking down there and for signs of a waterfall."

As Irwin made a slow circle, Josh said, "Hey! Kong and those men are walking right into the side of that mountain."

"There must be an opening there," Josh's father replied. "Maybe it leads to a small canyon or something."

Irwin said, "I'll swing over in the direction they disappeared so we can see where they come out."

Moments later, another valley, somewhat larger with sheer cliffs on all sides, slowly swam into Josh's view.

"You're right, Mr. Irwin," Josh said, pointing. "There's a very narrow canyon between those two mountains. Kong and the others are just coming into a second valley."

A rainbow suddenly appeared in front of Kong and the two men. "There's the waterfall!" Josh exclaimed. "The sun's making a rainbow of the spray. Kong and the others are heading straight toward it."

The pilot tilted the helicopter so that everyone could see. Forbidden Falls did not start at the top of the mountain like other waterfalls. Instead, it spurted out from the side of the mountain perhaps a thousand feet above the valley floor. A projecting ridge prevented the cascade from being seen except at a certain angle where the sun shone on it.

As the waterfall passed out of sight behind and below, Irwin said, "I imagine heavy cloud cover usually makes it even harder to see. Since the falls originate from underground, it must be fed by a lava tube.

"As you know, all these islands are of volcanic origin. Red-hot lava spewed up from the bottom of the ocean and gradually built each island. Kauai's the oldest. When lava flows downhill toward the sea, sometimes it forms a tube. Naturally, the outside cools faster, so it makes a crust. The lava inside continues to flow until it empties out of the tube."

Josh asked, "But how did this lava tube get so high up on the face of that mountainside?"

"Have you ever seen on television when the Big Island's erupting?" When they all nodded, Irwin continued, "Well, once I saw a tube spewing red lava several feet above the older, solidified lava. It looked like a giant water hose spurting red-hot lava out and down into the ocean."

"I saw that," Josh declared. "So I guess it's possible that the same thing happened here long ago. But how does the water get there today?"

"I can answer that, Son," Mr. Ladd said. "All volcanic rock is porous. That's why Hawaii has no lakes. Since it rains so much here, the water above the waterfall percolates down from the top and collects in some kind of underground pool. Then it flows into the other end of that tube and becomes a waterfall, landing in the valley below."

Josh glimpsed something in the valley some distance from the falls. "What's that on the right?" he asked.

"A heiau," his father answered. "It's not broken down like some I've seen."

"Maybe that's where they plan to sacrifice my daughter at noon," Redcliff said, his voice breaking.

Irwin said abruptly, "Your three people on the ground are going right under the base of the waterfall. There must be a cave or another lava tube back there."

"Watch to see if they come out," Melanie's father said briskly. "If they don't, that's where they're holding my daughter."

Josh barely breathed as he strained to see out of the helicopter which seemed to dodge in and out of clouds. Satisfied, Josh declared, "I don't think they're coming out."

When the others agreed, Irwin asked, "You ready to land?" As they nodded, Irwin glanced down at the map in

Redcliff's lap. "Here's where we are," he said, tapping lightly with his finger. "Mark it, please."

He added, "We obviously can't set down here where they could see us, so I've checked those other valleys, and decided to set down where Phelps did."

Josh gulped, remembering how close the overhead rotary blades on Phelps's helicopter had come to clipping the cliffs around the tiny valley.

If Mr. Ladd was concerned, he didn't show it. He asked, "Won't we be heard, Jay?"

"I don't think so," Irwin replied. "The sound of the falls should prevent that. Well, here we go."

Josh and Tank exchanged frightened glances, then Tank closed his eyes, squeezing them so tight his face puckered. Josh said a quick, silent prayer and tried not to panic as the aircraft slowly descended to the level of the mountain top.

Josh held his breath and fearfully watched the sides of the mountain slide by very slowly. He felt as though they were slipping down into a deep hole so narrow that if he stuck his hands out, they'd touch the sides.

But this was much more dangerous, because if one of the overhead rotary blades even touched the sheer green face of the volcanic mountain, they would crash.

Josh heaved a great sigh of relief as the chopper touched down on solid ground. He wanted to shout with relief. Instead, he reached over and gently shook Tank. "You can open your eyes now," he said.

Over the sound of the throbbing motors winding down,

Josh heard his father ask, "Does everyone remember the plan?" When they nodded, he said, "Jay, you watch for us to come running with Melanie. Then take off just as soon as we're all aboard."

As they moved away from the aircraft with its overhead rotary blades winding down, Josh saw Melanie's father glance at his watch. "It's coming up eight o'clock," he said in a voice thick with emotion. "We have about four hours to find Melanie and get her back here safely."

Josh told Tank, "That should be enough time."

"Yeah, *if* something doesn't go wrong."

All four people started running toward the place where Kong, Opu Nui, and Holo had entered the narrow canyon.

But Tank's last words echoed in Josh's mind: "*If* something doesn't go wrong."

Chapter Thirteen

THE HIDDEN WATERFALL

osh realized several things could go wrong, but he tried not to think of them. He followed his father, Tank, and Redcliff across the small valley and found an opening where Kong, Holo, and Opu Nui had exited.

Melanie's father, leading the way, said firmly, "From now on, no talking, but keep your ears open."

Everyone nodded. Then Mr. Ladd followed Redcliff in squeezing, one at a time, through the narrow opening. Josh was last. The sheer walls on either side rose about 500 feet toward the now overcast sky. The canyon floor varied from three to six feet wide. A small stream threaded its way along a muddy path that had obviously borne heavy foot traffic over centuries.

Old Hawaiian trail, Josh guessed. His father had told them that the ancient Hawaiians had traveled all over the various islands. They had found ways through lush valleys and over high ranges so that the shore dwellers and mountain people could exchange their goods.

127

Last night's rain storm had made the trail muddy and slippery, but the four people, moving without talking, made good time until Redcliff, leading the way, neared the light marking the end of the canyon. He held up his hand in silent warning for all to stop. Beyond him, about a hundred yards away past a sheer rock-faced mountain, Josh could see Forbidden Falls in all its splendor.

But as Josh's eyes traveled down the cascade to its base, he stiffened in alarm.

Holo and Opu Nui stepped out from behind the base of the falls. They had changed to colorful red and yellow uniforms with a military appearance, yet with a distinct suggestion of old Hawaii.

Holo and Opu were followed by a group of similarly dressed young men, including Kong. He looked the youngest, in spite of his bulk. Like most Hawaiians, the recruits were big, although Kong was even bigger. Josh saw some of them flinch as the swirling mists from the falls hit their faces.

There they halted in a single line, bringing their bare feet together smartly. Josh saw Holo's mouth move, but couldn't hear because of the waterfall. Opu and the youths turned sharply away, obviously in obedience to a command, and marched across the lush green valley floor, away from where Josh and the others crouched.

"What're they doing?" Josh asked.

His father answered, "They must be Pono Paha's Young Warriors getting ready to hold their initiation ceremony, probably at that heiau at the far end of the valley. Since that many couldn't have been brought in by helicopter, most must have walked."

"I wonder how come Kong got to fly in?" Josh asked.

"Maybe because he's so mean they were afraid to make him walk," Tank joked.

Redcliff was not amused. He scowled disapprovingly at Tank, then turned to look at the waterfalls. "There must be another lava tube or a cave behind those falls. They're probably holding Melanie there. I'm going . . ."

"Wait!" Mr. Ladd hissed. "There's somebody else moving right behind the falls."

Two men walked out of the mist. Each was at least six feet tall, barefooted, wearing only loincloths and carrying a spear and shield in one hand. With the other, they supported someone between them.

"Melanie!" her father cried, starting to step forward, but Josh's father held him back.

"Brad, wait! Rushing out there right now would be disastrous for all of us. We have to wait and find a way to save her."

Josh didn't see how that could happen. It seemed obvious to him that her captors were taking Melanie toward the heiau. There they would probably perform secret ceremonies, including initiating Kong and the other recruits into their organization.

At noon, Josh realized with cold dread, *they'll probably finish with Melanie as their sacrifice.*

Josh saw Redcliff's shoulders slump in despair as

Melanie was half-led, half-dragged away from the waterfalls. She wore a flowing white holoku* with an orchid and plumeria lei around her neck. Red and white ginger blossoms were woven as a crown about her head. Her face was pale, as her escorts supported her by both arms.

Suddenly, Melanie's head dropped forward, her legs folded, and she sagged to her knees.

"She's fainted!" Redcliff leaped up with a hoarse cry, but Josh joined his father in reaching out and hauling him back. He struggled, but Mr. Ladd clapped a hand over his mouth and held him down until he relaxed.

When Josh looked again toward Melanie, he saw one of her guards lay down his spear and shield. He picked up the girl's limp form and carried her back toward the base of the falls.

The other guard, still gripping his spear and shield, shouted something to Holo and Nui at the head of the column of boys. They had all turned to see what was happening behind them. They snapped to attention as Holo's mouth moved. Then the boys formed a single column and continued marching toward the distant heiau. Kong was the last one in line.

"Now what?" Tank asked.

"I don't know," Mr. Ladd replied, "but I'd guess they'll revive her and then bring her out again."

Redcliff's voice was thick with emotion as he commented, "John, I'm no fighter, and I doubt that you are, either, but right now it's just the two of them against us, and we have no weapons. However, we could use the spear that was left behind."

"I've never even held a spear, Brad."

"Neither have I, but my daughter's life is at stake. I'll take the spear. You coming?"

Josh wanted to cry out, "No, Dad!" but instead, he said, "Tank and I'll go with you."

Tank made a choking sound. "Josh, shouldn't we stay here and yell to warn your dad if somebody comes?"

"He'd never hear us above the waterfall," Josh pointed out. "So let's go."

"No," his father said firmly. "You boys had better wait here. If Brad and I don't get back before Opu and the others turn around, head for the chopper. If Brad and I don't come out in a reasonable time, you can conclude that we ran into trouble. So tell the pilot to take you boys out of here and radio for the authorities."

Josh nodded just as Redcliff started to step out of the shadowed crevice. He stopped suddenly as the two men reappeared without Melanie. One still had his spear and shield. The other retrieved his, then both jogged after the young warriors.

"Melanie's alone!" her father exclaimed. "Come on, John!" Redcliff bent low and darted out of the crevice ahead of Mr. Ladd. They ran toward the waterfall's base, keeping the cascading spray between them and the Pono Paha people.

Tank said excitedly, "Josh, I just thought of something. What if there's somebody else back there guarding Melanie? Maybe even the great Mano himself?"

"You're probably right," Josh admitted. "I doubt he'd miss this ceremony after the note he sent us."

Josh wanted to warn his father, who was following Redcliff. They had slowed their pace to pick their way across the wet, slippery rocks near the base of the falls, but they were too far away to hear Josh.

Suddenly, Mr. Ladd lost his footing on the wet, slippery rocks. He fell hard, but Melanie's father kept running, unaware of what had happened behind him.

Without thinking, Josh sprinted from his hiding place, followed by Tank. When the boys reached Mr. Ladd, he was sitting up, holding his right knee.

"Dad!" Josh cried, but the thunder of falling water was so great he could barely hear his own voice. Josh knelt beside his father and helped him pull up his right pants leg. After one quick look, Mr. Ladd motioned for the boys to help him up.

He stood on his left leg, but when he tried to put his weight on the right, it collapsed.

Josh slid his arm under his tall father's right shoulder and motioned for Tank to do the same on the other side. Supported by the two boys, Mr. Ladd hobbled to the canyon's entrance. They were far enough away from the waterfall so they could hear each other.

Mr. Ladd again pulled up his right pants leg.

Tank said hopefully, "Probably just a sprain."

Josh saw that the knee was already starting to swell. "Can you move it, Dad?"

He could, but it was obviously painful.

Josh said, "You can't walk on that."

"I've got to, son! Brad will need help bringing Melanie out."

"I remember my first aid course, Dad. If you walk on that knee, it'll make it worse. Besides, you're in no shape to help Mr. Redcliff. Tank, why don't you help him toward the helicopter while I go help Melanie's dad?"

Before Tank could answer, Mr. Ladd protested, "I can't risk letting you do that."

"Look, Dad, it'll take you awhile to get back to the chopper, even with Tank helping. So you go on, please. When Mr. Redcliff and I find Melanie, we'll have to run for the helicopter and hope the Pono Paha people aren't chasing us. It'll be hard enough to outrun them without having you hobbling along."

Reluctantly, Mr. Ladd nodded. "I don't feel right about leaving you...."

"I know, but we've got no choice," Josh interrupted. "Now, you two start for the helicopter. Make sure the pilot radios for the police. Tell them we've found Melanie, and to come fast. Tank and I'll get her and be right behind you. Be sure the pilot's ready to take off."

Josh cautiously picked his way across the slippery wet rocks to the base of the falls. There he pressed close to the wall to go behind the waterfall. He took a quick look toward the Pono Paha people. All of them had stopped at the heiau, still facing away from the falls.

Cautiously entering a high opening that led into darkness,

Josh realized that he was in an unusually large lava tube about ten feet high. His eyes probed the gloom ahead, but he couldn't see anything because of mist swirling about from the waterfalls. But, as he inched his way deeper into the tube, the mist was left behind.

In the darkness, he saw something. *Looks like a light,* he told himself. *Maybe that's where Melanie is. But where's her father?*

Knowing it was useless and possibly dangerous to call out, Josh eased forward again, seeking the source of faint light.

As he came closer, he realized there were several flickering lights placed along the lava tube. *Must be kukui nuts.** He had often seen the polished, dark walnut-sized seeds strung together as leis. However, he had never seen the oily nuts used for lamps, as the ancient Hawaiians had done.

The fluttering flames gave little light, but it was enough that Josh could pick his way in what would otherwise have been total darkness.

"Where *is* she?" he mumbled to himself. "And where's her father?"

Still inching forward, feeling his way by the rough interior of the lava tube, he had another terrifying thought. *I sure hope they haven't got an atom bomb stored in here. I wonder if it could be set off accidentally if I stumbled into it?*

Something moved in the dancing shadows cast by the kukui nut lamps. The sound of the falls grew less distinct as he worked his way into the depths of the tube. Josh's heart instantly raced, thumping against his chest and seeming to creep up in his throat so he couldn't breathe. *Mr. Redcliff?* he wondered. *Melanie? Or another member of the Pono Paha? Maybe Mano himself?*

Whatever had moved was near the bottom of the rough lava tube. Josh's frantic eyes slowly made out a white shape. Very cautiously, he slipped closer, then stopped when he caught a whiff of the sweet, heady fragrance of wild ginger blossoms. He remembered seeing them in the girl's hair moments before.

"Melanie?" he asked, his voice now barely audible and echoing in the tube. He knelt quickly. "Melanie?"

Her head had been down so her face didn't show, but she abruptly jerked her head up, causing her floral crown to fall off. She started to leap to her feet, then hesitated as light from a nearby kukui nut struck the boy's face.

"Oh, Josh!" she cried, throwing her arms about him and almost pulling him off balance. "I'm so glad to see you! How'd you get here?"

"Shh!" he cautioned, glancing around, grateful that he saw nobody else. "Helicopter," he added softly, then freed her arms from around his neck, breaking the orchid and plumeria lei. It fell free. Josh took Melanie's hands, pulled her to her feet. Then, still holding one hand, he started leading her back the way he'd come.

He stopped abruptly to again face her. "Where's your dad?"

His words made a hollow, echoing sound, disappearing down the tube while the flickering light from a kukui nut shown on her face.

"My dad?" she asked blankly, pulling the ginger blossom crown from her head and dropping it beside the lei.

She doesn't know he came in here, Josh realized. *No sense telling her.* Aloud, he said, "Never mind." His mind raced with sudden choices. *Should I try to find him? No, I don't even know where he might be if he's not in this tube. Right now, I'd better get Melanie out of here.*

He again took her hand and started pulling her toward the tube's entrance, feeling, more than hearing, Melanie's relieved or frightened sobs. He hurried on as the sound of the waterfall grew louder and the kukui nut lights were left behind. Josh could now see daylight at the tube's opening behind the falls.

We have to make it, Josh told himself, hurrying as fast as he dared. His thoughts jumped. *I hope her father's okay. My dad and Tank should be close to the helicopter by now.*

Curling tendrils of moisture from the waterfall settled gently on Josh's face as he neared the entrance to the tube. "We're almost there," he said encouragingly.

His heart had seemingly been trying to bend his ribs from the inside since he'd first probed behind the waterfalls. Now, as he left the tube and passed beyond the edge of the falls, he shot an anxious glance toward the heiau.

He was greatly relieved to see that all of the Pono Paha people were standing there. Their backs were no longer turned, but they didn't seem to notice any movement at the falls.

With the continual explosive sound of the waterfall drowning out all other sounds, the boy and girl began picking their way across the wet, slippery stones. A gust of wind shot a white spray from the falls over them, soaking their clothes. Melanie lifted her long holoku above her ankles for greater freedom of movement.

When they cleared the swirling mist and made their way along the wall, Josh's eyes flickered to the puka,* the opening of the tube. He pointed to it and raised his voice.

"Follow that canyon back the way you came until you see our helicopter. And hurry! My dad and Tank should be there with the pilot."

Melanie looked up at him with eyes swimming in tears. "What about you?"

He hesitated, then decided to tell her. "Your father went under the waterfall looking for you awhile ago. I've got to go back and find him before those guys come back."

"Daddy's back there?" Her eyes grew wide. "I'll go with you."

"No! You get to the helicopter." He started to turn back toward the falls. I'll find . . ."

Josh sensed someone behind him. He spun around to see an immense brown-skinned stranger rushing toward them.

Josh gave Melanie a little shove. "Run!" he cried.

She obeyed instantly, fleeing like a mongoose toward the opening to the canyon.

Josh whirled and dashed frantically after her, hearing the pursuer getting closer with every step.

Chapter Fourteen

FRANTIC EFFORTS

Josh and Melanie raced for their lives chased by the giant man. He was well over six feet tall and weighed about 300 pounds. He had dark curly hair, a shark's tooth necklace, a bare, hairless chest, and a loin cloth but no shoes. He carried a war club like those Josh had seen in a Honolulu museum.

For such a big man, the stranger ran very fast. Josh yelled, "Faster, Melanie! Faster! He's gaining on us!"

They had almost reached the entrance to the canyon when Josh glimpsed the tip of the war club as it was thrust between his ankles from behind, tripping him. He fell hard, rolling head over heels on the damp ground.

He lay there for a moment, partially stunned, but that didn't prevent him from seeing the pursuer overtake Melanie. He grabbed her right shoulder and spun her around, engulfing her in his arms. She screamed and beat uselessly upon his massive chest.

When she had stopped, he shoved her so she tripped over the train on her holoku and sprawled beside Josh.

The stranger spoke angrily to Josh. "Who are you?

How'd you get here?" When Josh hesitated, his captor yelled, "Speak up! I have no patience with haoles anyway, and especially for you who invaded this kapu place!"

Josh stalled, trying to think. He slowly got to his feet and tried not to let his voice betray the terror he felt. "I'm Josh Ladd. Who are you?"

The boy's name seemed to have no meaning to the giant. He said boastfully, "I'm called Mano," keli'i,* chief of the Pono Paha . . ." He interrupted his thought to stare at the boy. "You're Josh Ladd?"

When he nodded, Mano continued in obvious surprise, "Are you the same kid who's been running around the islands with another boy and two men, trying to find out about me and the Pono Paha movement?"

"Yes, because we were looking for Melanie," Josh explained, bending to where she was trying to get to her feet. "Are you okay?" he asked as she shoved the holoku's wet train aside.

"Just scared," she answered in a quavering voice.

"Never mind her," Mano commanded, jerking Josh to his feet. "Now tell me: how'd you get here? I captured one man, but there must be others. Where are the others?"

Melanie gasped. "You captured . . .?" She whirled to look up angrily at Mano. "You mean my daddy! Where is he? Is he hurt?"

"He's safe," the Pona Paha chief assured her, then added ominously, "for the moment."

The words sent a chill through Josh. He glanced at Holo,

Opu Nui, Kong, and the others running toward them. Josh's eyes lifted to the heiau beyond. *That's where we're going to end up,* he realized, *unless we can find some way out of this mess — and soon.*

Mano glared at Josh. "I'm going to ask you one more time," he said, again lighting tapping the end of the war club on Josh's chest. "Where are your friends? How many others are there? Speak up, haole boy!"

Melanie said stoutly, "Don't tell him anything, Josh! He'll never let us out of here, anyway."

"He'd better answer my question," Mano replied savagely, "or you'll never see your father again."

There was such coldness in the man's voice that Josh swallowed hard and tried to quiet his racing heartbeat. *Think!* he told himself fiercely. *Think!*

Josh didn't answer as the Young Warriors with Kong and their leaders arrived, breathless from their hard run. Kong's eyes opened wide in recognition. Josh doubted that the big bully had ever been so surprised in his life.

Mano motioned for everyone to be quiet and spoke sternly to Holo and Opu Nui. "What you two couldn't do in the last few days, I've done in a few minutes. The girl's father is tied up beyond the falls, and I caught this haole boy trying to escape with the girl."

The Pono Paha chief gave Holo and Opu Nui a disgusted look, then turned back to Josh and Melanie. "Since that puka is where you two were headed," he said, pointing to that canyon entrance, "it's obvious that you came that way. The means you had to have seen these two men arrive by helicopter with that big recruit. You undoubtedly followed them here.

"Now the only questions in my mind are how many people are waiting for you in your helicopter, and will they attempt a rescue?" He frowned thoughtfully, then answered his own question. "Well, it doesn't matter. We'll just speed up our ceremonies and be out of here before your friends can interfere."

Josh swallowed hard, fearful of what was going to happen to him, Melanie, and her father.

Mano turned to Holo. "Have one of your young recruits watch these two." Mano shifted his gaze to Opu Nui. "You bring the girl's father here so we can take them all to the heiau. Then both of you men come to my quarters. I'll get dressed for the ceremonies while the rest of these Young Warriors see how I deal with those who fail in their mission and allow themselves to be followed to this kapu place."

Josh saw the look of terror cross both Holo and Opu Nui's faces before Holo pointed to Kong who was standing closest in the line of recruits. "You look big enough to handle these two by yourself. Watch them."

Mano handed Kong the war club. "Take this. There's no time to bind these prisoners. Don't let them escape if you know what's good for you." Then Mano led everyone else back toward the base of the falls.

Melanie said with controlled fury. "Oh, that man is so terrible!"

"Don't think about that," Josh urged, glancing at Kong. He stood a few feet away, studying the entrance to the canyon. Josh lowered his voice. "We've got to figure out how to escape when they bring your father out."

"How can we do that?"

"The entrance to that canyon's only about 20 feet away. If there was some way we could distract Kong long enough to get in there, we might have a chance."

"Kong?" Melanie repeated. "You know our guard?"

"Yes. He's the neighborhood bully where I live. He loves to beat up on people smaller than he is. Anyway, if we could just get to that canyon, it's so narrow Kong would have to come at us one at a time. If we could just keep him back, or slow him down . . ."

"His club! Maybe you could grab it away from him before we run to the canyon. If he got close, you could bop him with that club."

Josh couldn't see himself bopping Kong, although the idea appealed to him.

"Let me think," Josh said, pulling up his knees and leaning forward to put his chin on them. "Ouch!" he exclaimed as the scholarship pin on his shirt poked him in the chest. "This is yours," he said, starting to unfasten it. "I found it where they kidnapped you, so I saved it for you."

"It's not important," she said, reaching out to stop him. "Only one thing's important now."

Josh nodded, swallowing hard. *Yes, to live*!

His gaze settled on Kong, who met his eyes and scowled.

"Dis place kapu to haoles," he said. "Why you come?"

"We found a note saying they were going to sacrifice Melanie here . . ."

Kong interrupted. "No sacrifice, you pupule malihini. Only ceremony."

Fearing what was planned when Mano and his men returned made Josh say something he never would have dared before. "You're wrong, Kong! Now you get stink ear. You don't listen well."

The big kid threatened, "You make Kong huhu!"*

"I don't mean to make you mad, but it's true. Now it looks as if her father and I will be killed with Melanie. At least, we won't be allowed to leave here."

Josh saw a change come over Kong's face, like a shadow of doubt. His jaw muscles twitched and his brown eyes darted from Melanie to Josh and back to Melanie.

Josh asked in surprise, "You really didn't know, did you, Kong? In your enthusiasm to join a hate group like the Pono Paha, you didn't dream how far they'd go. You probably thought that you'd just go around with that gang, bashing haoles, and take back these islands, didn't you?"

Kong didn't reply. He continued to stare, his face reflecting uncertainty and deep emotions.

Melanie whispered, "Careful, Josh. He'll hurt you."

Kong abruptly turned around and walked a few steps away.

Josh lowered his voice. "He's a bully, but I don't think he'd want to have any part of taking someone's life. He was just so proud of being invited to join the Young Warriors and go to Forbidden Falls that he probably never dreamed it was going to be anything but an initiation ceremony."

They watched Kong as he paced back and forth, ending up at the opening to the canyon. "You sure got him stirred up," Melanie commented.

Josh didn't answer but watched Kong with rising hopes until Melanie whispered, "Daddy!"

Josh turned to see Opu Nui leaving the waterfalls with Redcliff. His hands were bound behind his back. Kong quickly returned to stand in front of Josh and Melanie, thumping the club in his open left palm.

"Oh, Daddy!" Melanie cried, leaping up and throwing her arms about her father's neck, "Are you all right?"

"Just a little sore head from where their leader sneaked up and hit me from behind. What about you?"

"I'm okay, except for being scared to death."

Opu Nui said, "Keep an eye on this one, too, Kong," and hurried back toward the falls.

Josh turned to Kong. "Why don't you untie him so he can hold her? A father should be able to do that with his daughter at a time like this." When Kong shook his head, Josh taunted, "What's the matter? You afraid?"

"Kong not scared."

"Then prove it," Josh shot back.

With a rumbling growl like an animal, Kong roughly removed the supple green vines that bound the man's hands. He immediately encircled the girl in his freed arms and held her tight.

Josh turned back to Kong, leaving father and daughter a moment of privacy. "Kong, how come you hate me so much?"

"Kong and Mano hate all haoles same," Kong assured him. "For t'ousand years, maybe more, kanaka maoli live free. Swim, fish, raise taro,* banana, and chickens. Then haoles come. Steal land. Take all. Make kamaaina live like Indians on Mainland, only worser."

Josh was surprised at the vehemence in Kong's voice.

"I'm sorry about that," Josh replied. "The Hawaiian people I've met are wonderful. The authorities are trying to work this sovereignty problem out peacefully. So why can't you wait for that?"

Kong spat contemptuously at the ground. "Do dat, an' nothin' change. But Mano and Pono Paha make you haoles listen. Take back all dis place, Hawaii." He swung his arms in a wide, all-encompassing gesture.

Kong continued, his voice rising with anger. "Mano told Young Warriors how bad haoles treat him since little keiki-kane* living with tutu.* Haoles don't give her land dey promise. She die from sad. When Mano young kane, put in jail for steal. He get so huhu he make da kine plan for Pono Paha. Now, haoles pay. Big surprise soon. Den all haoles gone dis place. Only kanaka maoli left."

Josh genuinely felt compassion for Kong and his ancestors. "What's been done to your people and you isn't right, not right at all. I know the kanaka maoli movement has tried for a long time to get those wrongs corrected, but it hasn't worked."

He hesitated, thinking fast before continuing. "So I don't blame you for being angry and maybe even wanting to join with others who feel as strongly as you do. But are you ready to let three people die, Kong?"

"Kulikuli!"*

"I will not shut up! Under the law, if you take part in what Mano plans, you're as guilty as anyone else."

Kong brandished the club. "Mai oleo pela!"*

Josh hadn't ever learned the Hawaiian expression, but he could guess the meaning. "I *will* talk like that," he shot back firmly, ignoring the club. "You've beaten up on lots of boys who're smaller than you, but how many girls have you ever hit?"

Kong drew himself up proudly. "Kong not hit wahines."*

"I didn't think so," Josh said, hurrying to make his point. He dropped his voice to ask softly, "Then how can you let them take the life of this girl?" He added quickly, "What if she was your sister Kanani?"

With a strangled cry, Kong turned away. He stalked to the canyon puka and paused, his back to the others.

Josh exchanged glances with Melanie and her father. When Redcliff started to speak, Josh held up his hand, stopping him. Slowly, Josh turned to look at Kong's broad back, knowing that three lives depended on what happened next.

The silence stretched on for several seconds while Josh let Kong think it through. Finally he asked without turning around, "What you want Kong do?"

"Let us go."

"No!" Kong spun to face them, his eyes moist and bright. He started to say something else, then stopped at a faraway, haunting sound.

Melanie asked anxiously, "What's that?"

"Pu,"* Kong explained with a voice suddenly soft and strangely gentle. "Shell horn signal."

Melanie's eyes opened wide in fright. "Oh, Daddy! They're ready!"

In desperation, Josh demanded, "Kong, make up your mind! Are you going to let us go?"

Kong said in a frightened croak, "If Kong do dat, Kong dead."

Josh hadn't thought of that. He said the first thing that popped into his head. "Not if you come with us! You'll be safe then!"

Kong hesitated a moment, then nodded, motioning them toward the entrance to the canyon. "Go ahead! Hele!"*

With a glad cry of relief, Josh waved Melanie and her father to proceed him.

As Kong brought up the rear, they raced into the opening of the canyon just as the shell horn's haunting call came again.

At the same instant, Josh had a terrible thought.

Even if we make it to the helicopter, there's not room for all of us.

One of us will have to stay behind!

Chapter Fifteen

FINAL DESPERATE MOMENTS

Hotly pursued by the shouting, angry Mano and his radical Pono Paha followers, Josh raced on, following closely on Redcliff's heels. He was right behind his daughter, with Kong pounding along in the rear.

Josh quickly figured how many people the waiting helicopter would have to carry if the three of them reached the aircraft before their pursuers overtook them.

It holds six, including the pilot. He's waiting with Dad and Tank, so that's three, Josh thought. *When we landed there was also Mr. Redcliff and me. That's five, with room saved for Melanie. That's a full load. But with Kong, we'll have seven. Somebody has to stay behind.*

Josh twisted his head to glance at the pursuit party about a hundred yards behind. The entire band of recruits followed Opu Nui, Holo, and Mano single file into the narrow canyon entrance.

Mano ran ahead of everyone. He carried a long pole with feathers circling the top end. Kahili.* The word came to Josh. It was the sign of alii,* or royalty. He had seen kahilis placed like standards behind the thrones of the old Hawaiian royalty at Honolulu's Iolani Palace.

The chief of the radical Pono Paha movement still was barechested, but now he wore a magnificent red and yellow cape about his shoulders. Josh had also seen similar ones at the museum, called feathered mantles. The ancient Hawaiians had made them with feathers from certain birds.

Recalling the war club that Mano had handed Kong, Josh suddenly felt sure he knew what had happened to the priceless artifacts that Melanie's father had been planning to write about before his trouble started. Mano, chief of the Pono Paha, had stolen them.

Josh's heart was thudding like a big drum and his breathing was becoming rapid when Kong puffed up behind him. "Wikiwiki,* Josh."

"I *am* hurrying!" Josh protested over his shoulder. "But I can't go any faster." He glanced ahead at Melanie and her father. They were showing signs of tiring.

"Pono Paha got spears!" Kong reminded Josh.

He'd forgotten about those, but the muscles on his back tensed as he imagined one of them striking. Then he tried to reassure himself. *They won't use the spears because they want us alive. I hope!*

He started to tell that to Kong but stopped when he saw Melanie begin to stagger. This forced her father to slow and try to help her, so Josh also slowed.

Kong was still pounding along, his immense bare feet hitting the ground with thuds that reminded Josh of the giant chasing Jack in the beanstalk story. The ancient war club added to the resemblance.

Kong stepped on the back of Josh's heels. "Move, you haole boy!" he commanded.

Josh felt sudden indignant anger while squeezing as close to the canyon wall as possible. "Okay, pass me, but don't try to pass them." He jerked his head toward Melanie and her father. He had draped his daughter's left arm over his right shoulder. Both were trying to run again, stumbling and slipping on the muddy trail.

In passing Josh, Kong puffed, "When see you bumby,* Kong punch you' face!"

Josh was so startled that his immediate reaction was to laugh, but he didn't. *We're running for our lives, and that's what he's thinking about! I guess he's having second thoughts about helping us escape. Maybe he's the one who'll have to be left behind.*

Josh rebuked himself. *Don't think like that. Kong gave us this chance to escape . . . if we make it.*

A sound like distant thunder made Josh glance up. Several hundred feet straight up the sheer canyon walls, a narrow strip of sky showed that dark clouds had closed in, threatening heavy rain.

Lord, give me wisdom! Josh prayed silently, splashing through the shallow stream that coursed down the canyon floor.

Everyone was running more slowly now as weariness overtook them. Josh could hear Mano and the Pono Paha followers shortening the distance between them. The sound like distant thunder grew louder, filling the canyon, bouncing off the walls, but never fading into the distance.

From behind, Mano shouted, "Give up, all of you! There's no way to escape."

The four panting fugitives did not reply.

They were about halfway through the canyon when Josh saw Melanie stumble twice, regain her feet with difficulty and run on, staggering a little.

"Don't give up!" Josh called to her. "We're going to make it."

"I . . . I can't go much further." she puffed.

Her father said firmly, "You must, Melanie!" You must!"

Josh looked around desperately, wildly hoping for some idea that would help.

The path varied from a couple of feet wide to about six. The only way for the pursuers to attack was from the rear, and then only one at a time.

Josh knew that the greatest danger would come when the fugitives exited the far end of the canyon and ran across open ground toward the waiting helicopter. In the open, the Pono Paha warriors could spread out and swoop down on Josh and the others from all sides. They would be easily overcome before they reached the helicopter.

There's only one way to keep that from happening, Josh realized. *Somebody has to stay behind at the narrow end of the canyon after the others leave it. One person could hold off Mano and his men until we get to the helicopter. But who's going to stay behind and do that?*

Josh realized he already knew the answer.

The thought made his stomach churn, but once the decision was made, he turned his mind to thinking how to hold Mano and his followers back while the others ran for the helicopter.

Josh's eyes skimmed over the running trio in front of him to the narrow exit from the canyon. As the walls ended, Josh also glimpsed the helicopter nearby. He saw the overhead rotary blades start to turn.

Josh called encouragingly, "Just a few feet more and we'll be out of here! Keep going! The pilot's seen us! He's starting the engine!"

Melanie was within a couple steps from the entrance when Josh was again aware of noisy vibrations in the air. It became a throbbing sound distorted by the echoing canyon and valley walls. Josh wasn't sure it was really thunder, but he was too concerned with the problems at hand to positively identify what he was hearing.

He saw with great relief that Melanie had reached the canyon exit. It was so narrow that she had to quit running and squeeze through while her father dropped back a couple of steps.

As her father followed, Josh yelled, "Great! Run for the . . . Kong, what're you doing?"

Josh watched in disbelief as Kong squeezed his bulk through the opening, then roughly pushed Melanie and her father aside. They were thrown to the ground as Kong turned toward the waiting helicopter.

Josh shouted, "Kong, no! Come back here!"

He didn't answer, but threw the war club into the mud and kept running.

Josh pushed through the exit and bent to help Melanie and her father as they wearily struggled to regain their feet.

"Can you walk?" Josh asked anxiously, stealing a fearful glance at Mano and his warriors. When Melanie and her father nodded, too breathless to answer, Josh urged, "Then keep going. Get aboard fast. I'll be along in a minute." Silently, he added, *I hope!*

He ignored Redcliff's protests. "Go on, please!" Josh cried, giving the man a firm push on his shoulder.

As father and daughter again started running toward the waiting aircraft, Josh shot a fearful look back. Mano and his warriors were now within 50 yards and closing fast. Wildly, Josh snatched up the war club, knocked the mud from it, and turned to face the oncoming radicals.

Josh was not a fighter, for that was against his nature and beliefs. *But I'll do what I have to do,* he told himself, bracing his legs.

Resisting a stitch in his side, and ignoring the burning in his lungs, Josh had a momentary remembrance of something in the Bible about a man needed to stand in the gap. Josh also remembered Samson. He must have stood in some kind of sheltered spot like this when he slew a thousand men with the jawbone of a donkey.*

Mano and his warriors were now within fifty yards,

strung out in narrow file behind their leader.

Josh shot a quick glance toward the helicopter. The overhead rotary blades were spinning fast, ready to lift off. Melanie and her father were being helped aboard by Mr. Ladd and Tank. Josh closed his eyes, thinking this was the last time he'd ever see them.

The shouting of Mano and his men made Josh open his eyes. *Almost here!* he realized, feeling his mouth go dry with the terror of the moment. He caught a movement off to his right and turned to see his dad was out of the helicopter, limping toward him, accompanied by Tank.

Josh gasped, then yelled, "No! Stay back!" His voice was almost drowned out by the heavy sounds that now seemed to fill the canyon and bounce off the walls of the little valley.

Something whizzed by his head. Josh had never heard a spear thrown, but he instinctively knew what it was. He automatically ducked and whirled toward the onrushing warriors.

Holo stepped back, obviously having thrown the spear, while Opu Nui took his place. He drew back his arm to throw a spear.

Josh ducked down beside the canyon opening, making himself as small a target as possible. He saw Opu's arm stop in midair at Mano's sharp command. He looked up. All his warriors did the same.

Josh glanced skyward and let out a mighty yell. Overhead, military parachutes were popping open above the tiny valley in which Josh stood. Over the ridge, Army helicopters were settling down into the bigger valley where the heiau was. Heavily armed soldiers in full battle dress poised in the open doorways of each chopper.

"Whooeeee!" Josh yelled, dropping the war club and waving both hands wildly over his head. "It wasn't thunder I heard! That's the most beautiful sight I've ever seen in my life!"

* * *

At the Honolulu Airport, on the last day of the year, Josh, Tank, and Mr. Ladd waited for the Redcliffs' flight to the Mainland to be called.

Josh awkwardly watched Melanie as she fingered a vanda orchid lei* about her neck. "Thanks," she said, shyly smiling at him.

Josh didn't seem to hear. "Here," he said, extending an upturned palm. "This is yours."

She glanced down, then shook her head. "Thank you, but that scholarship pin really belongs to you. When school starts again next week, I'm going to tell the teacher that you really won it last year."

Tank, standing next to Josh, muttered under his breath, "She sure has changed."

Melanie turned thoughtful eyes upon him. "You're right. Nobody can go through what I did the last few days and still be the same."

Redcliff had been talking to Josh's father, but turned to the boys. "I'll never be able to thank you two for what you did for Melanie and me. Especially you, Josh, for staying behind alone to let us escape."

Josh squirmed uneasily, not knowing what to say.

Melanie's father added, "If you hadn't thought to tell your dad and Tank to radio the authorities when they got back to the helicopter, probably none of us would be standing here today."

Josh said, "It was the bomb that made the soldiers come. If they hadn't thought that Mano and his Pono Paha people were hiding a nuclear bomb at Forbidden Falls, I don't think they'd have come. At least, not in time."

Mr. Ladd said fervently, "Thank God they found it before it could be placed at an airport. But I guess the powers that be will never let us know for sure whether they found a nuclear device or just an ordinary bomb."

"It's easy to understand their reasoning in keeping that detail a secret," Redcliff commented. "It'd be too scary for people to know."

Melanie looked at Josh again. "I hope the problems over Hawaiian sovereignty are soon worked out, and everyone's satisfied."

"Me too," Josh agreed heartily. "But at least Mano, Holo, Opu Nui, and the rest of the Pono Paha group aren't going to be able to threaten anyone for a long time."

Tank grumbled, "I wish we could be sure the same was true of Kong."

"Kong may not change," Josh said, "but at least he did something that gave us all a chance to live. He'll probably be going around school, bragging about all the publicity he got."

Tank made a snorting sound of derision. "It's too bad the newspapers and television didn't tell about him running away and leaving you all alone! The way they told it, he saved everybody's lives by helping you escape."

"Well," Josh replied with a shrug, "I doubt that he'll be pulling on those black gloves to thump on us for awhile. That's good enough for me."

A uniformed airline attendance announced over the public address system that boarding was about to begin for the flight to Los Angeles.

"That's us," Redcliff said, shaking hands with Mr. Ladd, then Josh and Tank. "Thanks again."

Melanie looked somberly at Josh. "There's still one thing I still don't know."

"What's that?"

"Since you knew that I'd not been fair in winning that pin, plus all the other things I did to you and Tank back on the Mainland, why'd you do so much for me here?"

Josh shrugged but didn't answer.

His father explained, "I think my son and Tank did what they did because that's the kind of boys they are. That is, they saw something that needed to be done, and they did it."

Redcliff nodded. "Sort of like that verse you quoted me when this whole thing started, John. What was it? Something about doing good when it's within your power to do so?"

"Close enough," Mr. Ladd replied.

"Well," Melanie said, giving Josh a final smile, "Bye

now. Stay out of trouble."

Tank laughed. "Josh can't do that because trouble always seems to come looking for him."

After the Redcliffs' plane was airborne, rounding Diamond Head well out to sea, Josh thought about what Tank had said.

"Do you really think that's true?" Josh asked.

"I'm positive."

"What do you think will happen next?"

"I don't have the foggiest idea, but I'm sure it's going to happen."

"Well, at least I won't be alone, because you'll be with me. You always are."

"That's what scares me most," Tank replied with a laugh.

Josh joined in the laughter. He felt good as his father's old white station wagon headed toward home and the next adventure the boys knew was coming up fast.

GLOSSARY

Chapter One

Oahu: (Oh-WHA-hoo) Hawaii's most populous island and the site of its capital city, Honolulu. Oahu is Hawaiian for Gathering Place.

Honolulu: (hoe-no-LOO-LOO) Hawaii's capital and the most populous city in the 50th state is located on the island of Oahu. In Hawaiian, Honolulu means Sheltered Bay.

Aloha spirit: (Ah-LOW-hah) A loving attitude or friendliness.

Chapter Two

Waikiki: (Why-KEE-KEE) Hawaii's most famous white sand beach near Honolulu. Waikiki means Spouting Water.

Kahuku Point: (kah-HOO-coo) The most northerly spot on the island of Oahu.

Kaneohe: (Khon-ee-OH-hee) A major area on Oahu's windward (eastern) side near Kailua Bay.

Koolau Range: (koh-OH-lau [as in ow!] range) The volcanic mountains rising directly behind Honolulu.

Plumeria: (ploo-MARE-y-ah) Also called frangipani

161

(FRAN-gee-PAN-ee). A shrub or small tree which produces large, very fragrant blossoms. They are popular in leis.

Lanai: (LAH-nye) Hawaiian for a patio, porch, or balcony. Also, when capitalized, Lanai is a smaller Hawaiian island.

Mano: (mah-NO) Hawaiian for shark.

Pono Paha: (poe-no PA-ha) An Hawaiian expression meaning, "Is it right?"

Lilikuokalani: (lee-lee-OO-OH-Kah-lah-nee) The last of Hawaii's reigning monarchs, the queen was dethroned by show of U.S. military force in 1893. She is also famous for writing hauntingly beautiful songs of her people.

Kanaka Maoli: (kah-NAH-kah mah-OH-lee) True Hawaiians.

Sovereignty: (SOV-rin-tee) The supreme independent authority or power in a state or government.

Haole: (HOW-lee) An Hawaiian word originally meaning stranger, but now used to mean Caucasians, or white people.

Kamuela: (kah-muh-way-LAH) Hawaiian for Samuel.

Local: A term used in Hawaii to indicate people who are long-time area residents, but not necessarily kamaainas, or natives.

Chapter Three

Holo: (HOE-lowe): To run.

Opu Nui: (Oh-poo NOO-ee) Big belly.

Haleiwa: (holly-EE-vah) A community near the ocean on Oahu's north shore.

Iolani Palace: (ee-oh-LAH-nee) Once the only former royal palace used as the seat of an American government, the structure in downtown Honolulu is now an historic site.

Ku'o Ko'a: (KOO-oh KOO-ah) Independence.

Diamond Head: An extinct volcano and prominent Honolulu landmark.

Chapter Four

Aloha shirt: (ah-LOW-hah) A loose-fitting man's Hawaiian shirt worn outside the pants. The garment is usually very colorful.

Mynah birds: (MY-nah) An Asian starling that's dark brown and black, with bright yellow bill, white tail tip and white wing markings.

Be-still tree: A short, poisonous tree with dense green foliage and bright yellow flowers that fold up at night.

Kanani: (Kah-NAH-nee) Hawaiian for the pretty one.

You get stink ear: Pidgin for you don't listen well.

Pidgin English: (PIDJ-uhn) A simplified version of English. It was originally used in the Orient for communication between people who spoke different languages.

Malihini: (mah-lah-HEE-nee) Hawaiian for newcomer.

Da kine: (dah-kine) Pidgin English for "the kind." This is more of an expression and is therefore not usually translated literally.

Kapu Falls: (KAH-poo fahls) Kapu is an Hawaiian warning that means taboo, forbidden, or keep out. In this

163

story, the fictitious waterfall is forbidden to all haoles.

King Kamehameha: (Kah-may-HAH me-HAH) is also known as Kamehameha I or Kamehameha the Great. This famous Hawaiian chief conquered and unified the islands in 1810, established law and order, and began a royal dynasty.

Kaka-roach: (COCK-ah-roach) Hawaiian slang for theft or rip-off.

Hapa: (HAH-pah) Means half or part, as a person who is part Hawaiian.

Kamaaina: (kham-ah-EYE-nah) An Hawaiian word meaning child of the land, or native.

Lolo: (lo-Lo) Hawaiian for dumb or ignorant.

Pau: (pow) Hawaiian for finished, done, completed.

Sodbuster: American slang for a dirt farmer.

Mongoose: A small, agile carnivore imported to Hawaii from India long ago. It feeds mostly on birds' eggs and rodents.

Lunalilo Freeway: (loon-ah-lee-LOH) A section of highway running behind Honolulu.

Likelike Highway: (Lee-kay lee-kay) The name giving to Highway 63 which runs from Honolulu across the Koolau Range to Kaneohe.

Punaluu: (POON-ah-loo-oo) A small community on Highway 83 on Oahu's windward shore near Sacred Falls.

Kamehameha Highway: (Kah-may-HAH me-HAH) The same as Highway 99 beginning south of Haleiwa (holly-ee-vah) on Oahu's North Shore and running inland to Pearl Harbor with connections at Wahiawa (wha-hee-ah-wah) to the freeway known as H2.

Chapter Five

Antherium: (An-THEER-ee-um) A popular tropical, waxy-looking plant with heart-shaped bract which is a modified leaf although commonly mistaken for the flower. Antheriums vary from deep red to pink or white and sometimes even green. As cut flowers, they last for a couple of weeks.

Muumuu: (MOO-oo-MOO-oo) A loose, colorful dress or gown frequently worn by women in Hawaii. This word is sometimes mispronounced moo-moo.

Heiau: (HAY-ow) Ancient Hawaiian temple made of black lava pieces forming a rectangle. Some are raised like platforms.

Pele: (PAY-lay) The Hawaiian goddess of fire who supposedly caused volcanoes to erupt when she was angry.

Lauhala: (lau-HAH-la) Leaf from the pandanus tree used in making hats for visitors to Hawaii.

Kalakaua Avenue: (kah-lah-COW-ah) The main street running through Hawaii's famous Waikiki district.

Koolaus: (koh-OH-laus [as in ow!]) The common usage of the plural for the volcanic mountains rising directly behind Honolulu.

Chapter Six

Akaka Falls: (Ah-KAH-kah) A popular waterfall in

165

Akaka Falls State Park north of Hilo on the Big Island.

Waipio Falls: (Y-PEE-oh) A spectacular waterfall spilling from high cliffs into the ocean and visible from the Waipio Valley Overlook near the north east tip of the Big Island.

Kauai: (Cow-EYE) An Hawaiian island northwest of Oahu (where Honolulu is located). Kauai is thought by many to be the most photogenic of the islands.

Maui: (Mou (as in mouth) ee) The second largest island in Hawaii, it's slogan is "Maui no ka oi" (mou-ee no kah oh ee), meaning "Maui is the best." It ranges from the ocean to sugarcane and pineapple fields to mountains. These include the state's second highest rainfall area at Puu Kukui (poo-oo coo-coo-ee) with 400 inches a year, up to the 10,023 foot high dormant volcano called Haleakala (holly-AH-kah-lah, House of the Sun).

Waipio Valley: (Y-PEE-oh) A remote and primitive area available only by foot or four-wheel drive, starting at the ocean and going inland near the Big Island's north east end.

Waimea: (Y-MAY-ah) A community at the intersections of Highways 19 and 190 near the northern end of the Big Island. Kamuela is the post office. There's another Waimea on Kauai.

Kahuna: (kah-HOO-nah) An Hawaiian priest representing the ancient or traditional beliefs, or an expert.

Punchbowl: The common name for an extinct volcano rising directly behind Honolulu. Officially known as the

National Memorial Cemetery of the Pacific, it is the burial site for thousands of American servicemen.

Banzai Pipeline: (bhan-zye) One of the world's most spectacular surfing areas off Ehukai (eee-HOO-ky) Beach Park on Oahu's North Shore. Winter swells race across submerged coral in shallow water close to shore, causing immense waves that curl over and form a long tube through which only the most daring and skillful surfers attempt to ride.

Chapter Seven

Peka: (PEH-kah) Hawaiian for Bert.

Kunu: (coo-noo) Hawaiian for cough.

Kailua-Kona: (Ky-LOO-ah KOE-nah) An important community on the west shore of Hawaii's Big Island. It is almost directly across from Hilo on the eastern shore.

Chapter Eight:

Bougainvillea: (boo-gun-VEEL-ee-yah) A common tropical ornamental climbing vine with small flowers of many colors, including red, lavender, coral, and white.

Koi: (coy) Popular in Japan, these carp come in many brilliant colors. These fish are common in Hawaii's decorative pools.

Chapter Nine

Paniolos: (pahn-ee-oh-los) A word derived from the Spanish meaning Hawaiian cowboys.

Mauna Kea: (Mau-nah kay-ah) At 13,796 feet, this is Hawaii's highest mountain, or 119 feet taller than Mauna Loa. Both are on the Big Island of Hawaii. Kea means white in Hawaiian.

Malasadas: (Mahl-ah-SAHD-ahs) Round Portuguese pastries similar to doughnuts, covered with sugar, but without a hole. Malasadas are best when eaten hot.

Honokaa: (hoe-no-KAH-ah) A small community on Highway 19 near Waipio Valley on Hawaii's Big Island.

Hele mai: (HAY-lee my) Hawaiian for come here or come in.

Four-wheeler: A vehicle with power to all four wheels so it can go where ordinary cars and pickups cannot.

Lopaka: (loh-PAH-KAH) Bob or Robert.

Kapu: (KAH-poo) An Hawaiian warning that means taboo, forbidden or, keep out.

Kapunas: (kah-POO-nahz) Hawaiian for wise Hawaiian elders.

Chapter Ten

Tsunami: (tsoo-NAHM-ee) The Japanese word that in Hawaii means tidal wave.

Leprosy: (LEP-roe-see) The dreaded disease of Bible times that disfigures and causes loss of fingers, toes, and other extremities is now called Hansen's disease. It still exists, but is medically treatable. From 1866 to 1946, lepers in Hawaii were forcibly exiled to Kalaupapa. Some patients are still there, but their cases are arrested, so they are free to leave.

Kalaupapa: (Kah-lah-pah-pah) A very isolated, 4.5 square-mile peninsula on the island of Molokai's north shore. Kalaupapa is surrounded by immense ocean-facing

168

cliffs and fortresslike mountains.

Molokai: (MOH-low-ky) One of Hawaii's most unchanged islands, it's only 10 miles wide and 37 miles long. Two volcanoes formed the main island before a third volcano created Kalaupapa.

Kalalau Valley: (Kah-lah lou, as in ow) A spectacular, wide, green area surrounded by ancient volcanic ridges ranging up to the 4,000 foot high Kalalau Lookout which overlooks both the valley and the ocean.

Na Pali: (nah-polly) The cliff.

Mount Waialeale: (why-ah-lay-ah-lay-ah) The 5,148-foot-high mountain and extinct volcano that created the island of Kauai. It is the world's wettest spot, receiving between 500 and 600 inches of rain annually.

Chapter Eleven

Pupule: (poo-POO-lay) Hawaiian for crazy.

Lihue: (lee-HOO-ee) A small city that is the commercial and governing center of the Hawaiian island of Kauai. Lihue is also the site of the island's main commercial airport.

Lei: (lay). A flower garland. Visitors arriving or departing the islands are often given these leis to be worn about the neck.

Chapter Thirteen

Holoku: (HOE-low-COO) A dress with a long train which early missionaries developed to clothe native Hawaiian women. This garment became popular because it permitted wearers to run. The holoku has developed

169

into high style for modern Hawaii wearers.

Kukui nuts: (Coo-COO-ee) The nuts or seeds from this Polynesian import (now Hawaiian's official state tree) make beautiful shiny black leis. The nuts are rich in oil, so originally were burned as lights.

Puka: (poo-KAH) Hawaiian for a hole or opening.

Chapter Fourteen

Keli'i: (Keh-LEE-ee) Hawaiian for the chief.

Huhu: (hoo-hoo) Hawaiian for angry.

Taro: (TAR-oh) A plant grown throughout the islands for its edible, starchy roots.

Keike-kane: (KAY-kee khan-EE) A boy. Keike is Hawaiian for child and kane is masculine.

Tutu: (TOO-TOO) Hawaiian word for grandmother.

Kulikuli: (coo-lee coo-lee) Hawaiian for shut up.

Mai oleo pela: (My oh-lay-oh pay-lay) Hawaiian for don't talk like that.

Wahines: (wha-HEE-nees) Hawaiian for females or women.

Pu: (poo) Shell horn

Hele: (HAY-lay) Hawaiian for go come or walk, as: go ahead.

Chapter Fifteen

Kahili: (Kah-HEE-lee) An ancient Hawaiian emblem of royalty consisting of a staff or shaft, with one ending looking like a big red and yellow feather duster. A commoner seeing someone approaching carrying a kahili was required to lie face down so that the royal person would not be defiled by a commoner's shadow, gaze, or touch.

Alii: (Ah-lee-HEE) Hawaiian word for native royalty.

Wikiwiki: (WEE-key WEE-key, but commonly mispronounced as wicky-wicky by malihinis) Meaning hurry or quickly.

Bumby: (BUM-bee) Pidgin for by and by or after awhile.

Donkey: This incident in the life of Samson is found in Judges 15:15.

Vanda orchid lei: (van-dah or-kid lay). A flower garland of small orchids which grow wild in Hawaii, even in Honolulu. Visitors arriving or departing the islands are often given these leis to be worn about the neck.